Found Together

Book 2 of the Inked Together series

Diane Michaels

ArrowHeart Press

ArrowHeart Press

First paperback edition: March 2022

ISBN 978-1-7374156-3-3

CONTENTS

MONDAY

CHAPTER 1
ANJA

I most certainly did not agree to this. To have an eardrum-shattering air-raid siren yank me from a deep slumber is unconscionable. For it to occur at six in the morning? Yeah, no.

"Did you mean for that to happen?" I ask Colton, my voice more gravelly than a quarry. I roll toward him and present a pair of puckered lips desperate for a bit of soothing.

He exits the bed without giving my mouth its due. "People with real jobs get up early."

In case the alarm hadn't done its trick, his words shake the last vestiges of sleep from my brain. I prop myself on my elbows. "I have a real job, thank you very much."

His nose lifts and draws an arc away from me while he enjoys a laugh at my expense. "Writing publicity materials for classical musicians doesn't count. I am part of the world economy. People entrust me with their fortunes. My job matters."

"Music matters. Try going a day without listening to music."

"The world runs on popular music. Classical music is dead."

For want of energy, I refrain from throwing the lamp at him. "Not hardly. Imagine a *Star Wars* movie without its score. You can't, can you?"

"Anja, I don't have time to argue. I have to be at my desk in Lower Manhattan in an hour." He slips into the bathroom before I can offer my rebuttal.

The hiss of water flowing through his pretentiously oversized rain shower head stands in for his final word. I grip the top sheet and blanket and pull them to the base of my neck. I had higher hopes for this morning.

Last night was my first school night sleepover with Colton. Big step, right? Finding a guy who didn't shun a weekend sleepover early in the relationship was itself a major milestone. I came over last night prepared to match him, step-for-step, in his pre-work rituals.

My plan involved adding *sexy* to each task. Sexy good-morning kiss after my phone chimed its soothing alarm at a civilized decibel level and hour. Sexy shower. Sexy wearing of his dress shirt to make coffee. Sexy kiss goodbye at the point where our paths diverged en route to our offices. Sexy dash back into each other's arms because parting had become unbearable. Topped with a sexy laugh at how nauseatingly adorable we are in our new coupledom.

New is the operative word. We met twenty-three days ago. Though our post-wake up exchange was testy, it doesn't qualify as our first fight. We still have loads to learn about each other. Now I know he's an early riser who takes the whole "going to work" thing way more seriously than me. So be it. I can adapt. I *will* adapt because he's a good guy. A guy with serious boyfriend potential who deserves a reward—an image—to take with him to his fancy office.

Girlfriend in the kitchen, brewing a pot of coffee while wearing his shirt and nothing else? Weekend Colton has been a fan. I bet Monday morning Colton is, too.

I lean over the edge of the bed to grab the shirt he discarded in haste last night when being in bed together was the opposite of combative. My wingspan might be long enough to qualify me for the WNBA, but the shirt lies just beyond reach. Counting on my exhalation to propel me farther into the room, I fill my lungs and heave myself toward the shirt.

The bedding becomes a fishing net, ensnaring me and dangling my body over the side of the bed. I shrug my hand free to have another go at the shirt. The motion deposits me onto the carpet with a thud.

"What are you doing?"

Colton casts a shadow over me. Wrapped in a navy robe and with his damp brown hair styled to perfection, he's the ideal companion to my man's shirt-clad sexy self. Well, the fantasy version of me I had conjured a minute ago, not the trapped mermaid version sprawled across his hardwood floor.

"Things didn't go according to plan."

Once I've disentangled my left foot from the covers and wrapped myself in the top sheet, I attempt to restore order to the blanket and bedspread.

Colton bats his hand at me. "Don't bother. The maid comes today. You're more than welcome to lounge in bed as late as you wish."

"Since I'm awake, I thought I'd make us coffee."

He shakes his head. "No, thank you. I'm out of here in fifteen minutes."

"But—"

He kisses the top of my head. "You're sweet to offer. And you look good enough to eat. But work and…" He flicks his eyebrows to punctuate his inviting smile. "You're a powerful distraction, young lady. The thing is, the day I have in front of me doesn't leave room for distractions. Most weekdays are like this. Don't take it personally. You belong to my after-work life. You feel me?"

My hands very much would love to slip inside his robe to feel him. Mmm, abs. And…

Snap out of it, Anja. Be the perfect girlfriend.

"I should have understood your mornings would be more structured on weekdays. Sorry to derail your schedule."

He pulls a suit from his closet and lays it on the bed. "No prob. I shouldn't have said your job doesn't matter."

"We're in different fields. I wouldn't expect you to understand what my career entails."

We are rocking it with the conflict-resolving language. Our minor hiccup from earlier exits the building.

He slips his arm into his jacket. "You're right. You have the perfect job for you, or who you are right now."

Cue the needle scratching a record. "And who am I?"

"I shouldn't get into it right now." He sighs and takes a step toward the mirror, but reconsiders. "You're kooky, free-spirited. I appreciate your quirks. But not always. Friday, for instance, I'll need you to be someone different. You know what I mean, right?" He doesn't wait for me to scrape my jaw off the floor to answer him. "For the client dinner, I need you to play the part of the sort of person I'd, uh… the sort of woman whom they'd expect me to be dating. I thought you knew I was looking for a corporate wife. I bet you have it in you. It's time you introduce her to the world."

My Venus-on-the-half-shell ensemble, courtesy of his bedsheet, no longer matches my mood. I hitch it under my chin. "Asking a person, point blank, to change to meet your ideals will never make either of you happy. I'm sorry I'm not the woman you need me to be, Friday or ever. It was fun while it lasted, I suppose."

I scrounge for last night's outfit and head for the bathroom. I scrub my teeth harder than my dental hygienist would sanction and spit into the sink. It would have been more satisfying to have spewed the foam into his face, but I'm a lady, regardless of whether he recognizes it. I shove my limbs through the appropriate leg and armholes; hook, button, and zip where needed; and de-snag the worst my long blond hair has to offer. I'll fix the rest of this mess at the office.

Had I known he was searching for a cookie-cutter wifey doll before this morning? I swear, although he is devastatingly handsome—not to mention intelligent, emotionally stable, and generous—I wouldn't have fallen for a man who wanted to change me. It's one thing to adapt to his routine. It's an entirely different kettle of fish to become a person I am not. The thing is, the game of finding the man who lives up to his potential and who appreciates who I am is getting old. And so is living without him.

CHAPTER 2
GRIFFIN

S even words, not one of them wasted. Is my sister so confident I'll drop everything to return to a life I left behind five years ago that she doesn't need to waste a second selling her proposal to me? I shake my head before rereading the text.

I need you in LA. Come today.

Why she needs me is no mystery; she has previously hinted I could be useful. To which I replied I'd be as useful as a garden hose in a swamp. I see no reason for me to expand my carbon footprint by flying to the West Coast to assist in a job already well-managed. I stretch my fingers and prepare to mount my defense.

Can't. Have an appt this evening.

No way I'm sacrificing my tattoo appointment to muck around with packing the contents of a dying PR firm. It's not even my sister's company. Sure, I put in a couple of years on staff, but what special skills do I possess to make it worth my while to return?

> **Daphne:** We have a research-based project with your name all over it.

> **Griffin:** Since my name is all over it, what's left to research?

I crack myself up. Her, not so much. My ringing phone startles me. I sometimes forget these things aren't just for texting.

"When have I ever asked you for a favor?"

"Nice to hear from you, too, Daphne. How's the weather?"

"Low seventies, rising to a high of eighty-four. A darned sight better than Jersey City, I assume."

"I'll take changing seasons over your homogeneous weather any day. What do you smug Left Coasters have that's better than an early fall day, anyway?"

"While I'd love to spend hours dissecting the pros and cons of the meteorological regions of the United States, I called for another reason. We're drowning in files. I wouldn't have asked, but with the team focused on helping our current clients transition to new representation, the boxes in the middle of the floor containing content from our former clients have become tripping hazards. Somebody needs to track down to whom we should send the materials."

"Sounds like a job someone should have performed after your office stopped representing the clients."

"I won't argue with you, but the point is moot. No reason to blame a nameless member of the staff from forty, fifty years ago."

"Then throw everything away. If no one has noticed the files missing for decades, who wants them now?"

"It's not your call. The boss wants you to work your magic to unearth the rightful owners of the files."

"The boss, huh? None of this plan is your way of forcing me to visit you?"

"She asked me to recommend a researcher to spend four or five days searching for our mystery clients. I mentioned you, and she flipped."

"Clearly, she is not in her right mind to make hiring decisions, then."

"I've known you for twenty-nine years. I recognize your tactics. Humor is your favorite distraction technique once you've run out of arguments. What's preventing you from hopping on a plane this afternoon? Your self-inflicted daily word count?"

"I support myself by writing four thousand words a day. Besides, I've already told you I have an appointment."

"I'll buy you a ticket for a redeye tomorrow."

"What's in it for me to set my alarm for a ridiculous hour and perform a job I quit five years ago in a city I've made it my mission to avoid?"

"Excellent! I'll send you the flight details."

I bang my head against a kitchen cabinet. I gave in too early. "You didn't answer my question."

"But I won, right?"

"Don't you always?"

"Thank you for acknowledging my perfect record. We'll pay you, of course."

"I have additional conditions: I stay with you."

"You'd better stay with us. The kids can't wait for your visit. They're plotting a week's worth of games and stories as we speak."

Even my niece and nephew knew I was coming before she had asked me.

"I have the impression free will is an illusion," I say.

"I've always known you were smart. What else?"

"No restaurants or outings of any variety. I'm either at your house or in the office. Oh, and nobody beyond the obvious is to know I'm in town."

"Easier done than said. Who better than your favorite sister to roll out the red carpet for the world's biggest curmudgeon?"

"My least favorite sister. Get lost, will you? I have to mitigate the damage you've inflicted by torpedoing this week's schedule."

"I love you, too! Safe flight."

"Hmm."

I mash my middle finger against the red button on my phone's screen. A trip to LA means reworking today's plans. I have to find a moment to visit a toy store before I leave so I can buy the most annoying electronic gifts for my niece and nephew. Since Daphne plans to ruin my week, the least I can do is to disrupt the peace in her home long after I'm gone.

My phone rings again. I'm ready to throw it down the disposal until I catch the name of the caller.

"Hello?"

"Hey there. Are you Griffin?"

"Yes."

"This is Amber from Inklyn. How's it going?" she asks, her voice rising with friendliness. My heart rate accelerates.

"Fine."

"We're stoked you chose us for your next tattoo. Or is it your first?"

I imagine a woman standing behind a counter, twirling her finger around a strand of dark, wavy hair cut in a pageboy. Her Doc Martens and an array of tattoos project a goth vibe in balance with her bubbly personality. She sounds alluring, the sort of woman I'm not prepared to meet.

"My first."

"Right. We have you matched with Curly for your five o'clock appointment. He's the best. Do you have any questions?"

"No."

"All right. We'll see you later. Have a great day!"

I end our call without saying goodbye. She probably found my terse replies rude, which wasn't my intention. I'd give anything to carry on a conversation with a woman the way I can with my sister. But given the strikes I have against me, I'd be wishing for a miracle.

CHAPTER 3
ANJA

"You guys! How does this keep happening?" I pound the sides of my fists against the table at a local deli.

My best friends Violet and Tracey regard me with sympathy across from me at our favorite booth. Well, Violet does. Tracey heaves a sigh. "You called an emergency lunch meeting because of a guy?"

"I swear, Colton had serious potential. Hot, employed, and with no apparent fear of commitment. He introduced me to his friends over brunch a week after we met. Brunch!" I widen my eyes for emphasis.

Violet rolls the edge of the paper under her sandwich between her thumb and middle finger. "What happened? Does he suffer from a raging case of halitosis? Did he collect stray hairs from your brush and add them to his secret stash? Does he have a doll fetish?"

"Ding, ding, ding!" I tap my nose.

Tracey swishes a mouthful of soda, covering her mouth to prevent it from spewing when she swallows. "Um, gross."

"My bad. He doesn't have a doll fetish, per se. He wants to date Corporate Wife Barbie."

Violet's brow creases. "It may be a tad early to talk marriage, but it's a good sign he's on the marriage track, right?"

"I'm into having a hypothetical conversation concerning marriage and kids, but he took it someplace else. The nineteen-fifties, to be specific. While he appreciates that I am, in his words, 'kooky and free spirited,' what he's banking on is for me to ditch my disposable, unimportant career after I become a proper wife he can introduce to clients."

Tracey's upper lip curls. "Ugh. I hope you wiped your hands clean of the patriarchal mouth breather."

"Done. Changing into someone I am not was a deal-breaker. Too bad, because he was *hot*."

"No disrespect, but if all you want from a man is a piece of arm candy, why can't he ask the same of you?" Tracey chomps on a potato chip and raises her brow in a manner more self-satisfied than I care for.

"Oh, aren't you a fount of wisdom?" I scrunch my nose at her. "Can't I want a guy who is hot, fun, in it for the long haul, and appreciates me the way I am? I bring a lot to the table, and I'm ready to feast with the right partner. Remember our pledge from last month? Violet promised to quit her job and find a better one, I swore I'd date worthy men, and Tracey said she'd start dating again." Being an overachiever, Violet took her pledge to the next level and not only landed an amazing job, but a boyfriend to boot. "Violet, I'm not jealous of you for your bonus achievement of falling in love with Ben. Quite the opposite. Your relationship inspires me. Don't you agree, Tracey?"

She inhales sharply. "I'm super happy for you, Violet. Ben seems perfect. I have a groove going with my single life, though. I'd hate to ruin it by dating another man like…"

Tracey's ex could very well have been named Voldemort or Beetlejuice or insert your name of choice, where even uttering it out loud is akin to summoning the devil. I don't know which is worse; one man irreparably breaking your heart or my situation, which involves death by a thousand cuts.

Violet sets her mouth in a firm line. "I'm not so naïve to believe Ben is perfect, but I have a decent grasp of who he is. Sure, I'm lucky to have met such an awesome person, but we dug into the meaty topics before we even kissed. If you're intent on finding The One, wade through the uncomfortable conversations right away. Knowing a guy well is a way bigger turn-on than the physical stuff."

I nod. "Yeah, your method sounds smart, but I can't imagine asking the cute guy who offers to buy me a drink what his views on gender roles in a marriage are or whether he expects me to change my personality to suit his tastes. Wouldn't it be cool if men came with voiceovers that provided a recitation of the possible side effects of dating them the way they list them in TV commercials for IBS or ED? 'Prolonged exposure to this hottie may cause a hideous case of insecurity. Don't combine with carefully planned activities.' It could save me a heck of a lot of time and frustration."

"Looking for love has a way of blinding us, at least if you go in with an agenda and are willing to rule out potential matches based on whether they immediately sync with your requirements. You could try leaving the search for the right man to chance. Ben and I ran into each other at a tattoo gallery, and…" Violet glances upward, tapping her lip. "…and fate stepped in."

"Ooh, I'm glad you mentioned your tattoo story. I've been jealous of your gorgeous violets, and I seriously need a pick-me-up. I've made an appointment to get a tattoo tonight."

Violet cocks her head. "Where?"

"Inklyn. That's where you went, right?"

"Uh, yeah." She draws out her words, narrowing her eyes.

"They've matched me with a woman named Amelia."

She chokes on her water. "Sorry. Went down the wrong pipe. She's, yeah, I mean, she's talented. No, I'm glad she's tattooing you."

"Man, I'm going to be the loser in our group without a tattoo," Tracey says.

"Come with me. Maybe they can fit you in."

Tracey presses into the back of her seat. "You know how much I hate needles. I doubt there is enough room at the tattoo shop for the team of psychologists I'd bring with me to talk me off the ledge." She bats her hands. "Enough about my phobia. What kind of design are you getting?"

"A small butterfly on my ankle."

"Not in black, I hope," Violet says.

I gently punch her shoulder. "Silly. Me with a black tattoo? Gimme all the bright colors. Still, what's wrong with black?"

"Nothing. If you have to pick a shade of black for the outlines, go with a less bold shade than the black on my arm. You wouldn't want to overshadow the colors."

"Good advice. Thanks. I'd better run back to the office before anyone notices I'm missing. I'll text pictures of the finished tat later. You guys are the best. I've already forgotten about whatshisname."

CHAPTER 4
GRIFFIN

The dread of returning to LA clamps around my brain, throttling my creative and motivational centers. If spending five days in my least favorite place in the world isn't bad enough, struggling to make use of the last remaining hours I have before my trip is a greater insult than I can stand.

Some would claim I'm lucky to make a living writing steampunk novels, but it takes more than luck. Fans remain fans only as long as I give them new words to read. Since hitting my stride three years ago, I churn out eight books each year, which means I am always writing one novel, editing another, and preparing to launch a third. I have no hope of escape from this circus.

Not that I need to escape. I do best with a job whose description requires me to sit alone in a room, a skill at which I excel. And, with ideas for plots coming at me at a fast and furious pace, I envision a long, happy future in my chosen career.

I type a sentence before hitting the delete button. The words I had put into the head of Talib, my protagonist, are one hundred percent mine, not his. He is nineteen and full of an adventurous spirit. Never would he wish for the world to move forward without him.

I shove my chair backward and abandon my laptop. No point in driving myself nuts. I'll save the torture for Daphne.

I rub the bumpy skin on my right forearm, contemplating what to do next. "Big day for you, becoming the foundation for a work of art," I say to my arm.

The dotted line of shiny scars leading from the crease of my wrist toward my elbow has never lacked a certain element of beauty. The scars on my arm aren't the ones I need to beautify, but no way am I tattooing my face.

Ever since I recognized the similarity between the pattern and shapes on my arm and the black dots from Joan Miro's Blue II painting, I've dreamed of having a tattoo artist ink me to match. And in four hours, I'll make my dream come true by tattooing a black dot above each scar and punctuating the line with an amorphous red shape at the end.

I pour myself another glass of water. Hydration is key to healing. Or so they say. I set my phone on the kitchen counter. It gives me a raspberry in the form of a text notification.

> **Mallory:** Hey, stranger. Ran into Daphne. She mentioned you were coming to our fair city tomorrow. Wasn't aware you had left it. Which proves it has been way too long since we spoke. Text me when you're here. I'd love to catch up with you.

My heart stutters. I've heard neither hide nor hair from Mallory since two weeks before my accident. To say she played a role in why I was unreasonably drunk that evening would be an understatement. I've spent five years convincing myself I never need to hear from her again.

Based on the way my heart behaves upon reading her number, I haven't done a good job.

My fingers shake while I stab my pointer into the space where my reply belongs. The smiley face emoji on the right side taunts me. I slam the phone on the counter without replying.

I didn't need a blatant reminder that my trip to LA will put me unacceptably close to my ex. Especially a reminder delivered as an uninvited text from Mallory. Before I've even left my apartment, my sister has broken one of the cardinal rules behind my visit.

Over the last five years, I've built LA into an antagonist worthy of a spot in a novel. It wasn't always my enemy, and, in all honesty, it still isn't. I loved the four years I spent at UCLA. My sister had suckered me into becoming her assistant at the publicity firm, and despite the vast gulf between the entertainment industry and my interest in it, I didn't hate my job. It's not LA's fault my life changed. But a world built around appearances wasn't the place to be afterwards. I needed to leave, and fast. Returning to New Jersey, where I had lived in my childhood, gave me the cover I craved.

So, why the hell did I let Daphne talk me into returning to LA? And what business is it of hers to spill the beans to my ex?

CHAPTER 5
ANJA

I'm having trouble imagining Violet, the Queen of Neat and a champion planner, inside Inklyn Tattoo Gallery, let alone making the spontaneous decision to ask for a tattoo. Bold actions are more my style. Yet my heart is thumping a thousand times per second while I wait for my tattoo appointment. I lean against the reclaimed wood reception desk, hoping the receptionist doesn't notice my flop sweat.

"Amelia is on her way," he says.

"Great. Great, great."

"First tat?"

"Yes, sir. You've been down this road once or twice before, I see." I scan the sleeve of black, red, blue, and green ink covering his right arm.

He drags his T-shirt's sleeve upward to expose his shoulder and points to a faded American flag. "Got my first for my fifteenth birthday." He drops the sleeve, letting his fingers gather the hem of his T-shirt in front of his belly. "Wanna take a tour?"

The glint in his eye triggers another adrenaline rush. I suspect his offer has less to do with his pride in his ink than with his interest to get naked with me. He's definitely the antithesis of Colton, but that doesn't mean he's the right guy for me, either.

"I'm good, thanks."

"Anja?" A tiny woman with blond hair as pale as mine—except for four inches of cherry-blossom pink at the ends—crosses the room and extends her hand to mine.

"In the flesh. Are you Amelia?"

"Yup. You ready?"

"Ready as I'll ever be."

"You're good. I haven't killed anyone. Yet. Follow me."

We descend a metal spiral staircase, our clanging footsteps echoing against the walls. The stairs deposit us into a brightly lit room with eight tattoo stations. A classic rock song I've heard my father tunelessly sing along to blares through the sound system.

"Sorry to stick you in Grand Central, but the back room, which is quieter and decidedly less testosterone-filled, is at capacity. Take a seat."

I hop onto the lone unoccupied chair. A quick scan of the room confirms Amelia's point. We alone represent team estrogen. Were I here to select the future Mr. Lund, I'd like the odds. But I'm here for me.

"Butterfly above the ankle, was it?"

"Uh, huh. Is it super cliché?"

"Clichés exist for a reason. Nothing wrong with sharing a popular aesthetic. I've selected a few beautiful designs for you. Have a look."

Amelia hands me her tablet. I swipe pages ferociously, well practiced in the art of selecting the prettiest candidate on a screen. My heart commands my fingers to take a break when I reach the image on the fifth page. The vibrant peacock-blue on the upper half of the butterfly's wings fades to pale aqua between lines of black. On the lower portion, the sea foam-green on the outer points of each segment bleeds into white, which I assume will be un-inked patches of skin. The midnight-black border leaves dots of skin peeking through. Under the wings, pale gray smudges create shadows. The butterfly appears poised to flutter away without warning.

"This, please." I reach across the chair to hand her the tablet, reluctant to let go of it.

"Gorge. Show me your leg."

I roll my right foot inward and point to my ankle. She presses two fingers into the soft bit between the tendons three inches above the ankle bone. "Since it's your first, we'll avoid going near anything too painful, which means your butterfly will be perhaps an inch, inch-and-a-half in diameter. Sound good?"

"Whatever you say. You're the pro."

"I got you. While I print the stencil, pick two blues and a green."

She waves her hand in front of four glass shelves on the wall behind me. Like polish in a nail salon, a rainbow's worth of inks line the shelves. A bottle of blue calls to me. A shade lighter than cobalt, it radiates brightness and serenity. I hold it against the lighter blues until I find its best match. I set the two bottles plus a bottle of sage green on the metal tray and hop onto the chair.

Amelia returns and examines my colors. "Nice choices. I have *the* perfect black for you. I swear, I've never used a smoother, darker color of ink."

"A friend mentioned I might want more of a washed-out black to make sure the colors pop."

With her back toward me while she fumbles around in the cabinet below the shelves on the wall, she says, "Dude, who's the pro here? I promise you the contrast will be superb. Provided I can find my ink."

She removes her head from the cabinet, inserts two fingers between her lips, and lets loose a universe-rending whistle. "Yo, who's been in my stuff? I had a secret stash, and now it's missing. If I don't have my bottle of Magic

Mate Double Black in the next thirty seconds, heads will roll."

Half the tattoo artists ignore her. A few casually glance over their shoulders before returning to their clients. A man with a ZZ Top-level gray beard picks up a bottle from his workstation. "Sorry, Amelia. Saffron mentioned she had given you this ink. I figured, since I knew about it, I could use it."

"You figured wrong, Curly. Gimme."

"I don't need much more to finish my client's design. Can we share?"

"I never learned how to share. Bring it here. Now."

Curly tips the bottle over a white paper cup, squeezing out a last helping for himself before walking across the room. "Will a six-pack make things right?"

"No. Make it a bottle of Jameson, and we'll be even."

"Fine."

He returns to his station with a huff. Amelia waves the black plastic bottle in my face. "Best. Ink. Ever. Trust me. Let's get it in you."

She cleans my skin, applies the stencil, and steps away. "Is it okay?"

I bend my knee to examine my leg. "Groovy. Will the process make me scream at you like a woman in labor screams at her husband?"

"Won't bother me a bit. You handle the experience however you need. I'll give you a taste of the needles first. You comfy?"

"Aye, captain."

She pats my calf. The whine of the tattoo machine is worse than a horde of thirsty mosquitos. "Three, two…"

A twinge I'd place at one-point-five on the pain chart hardly even raises my eyebrows. "Mother trucker!" I yell, slapping my open palm against the edge of the seat.

She holds the gun aloft, and her eyes widen. "That bad?"

"No, just messing with you. Give me all you got."

The stinging disappears each time she pulls the needles from my skin. Left in their wake is a pleasant, sort of caressing sensation. I slip into a decent headspace, enduring the experience while Amelia talks to me.

"Has anyone ever told you that you look like Amanda Seyfried?" she asks.

"I've heard it before. Super flattering, though."

"You must spend half your life fighting off suitors."

"I spend half my life regretting my choice of suitor."

"The struggle is real. Well, not for me. Happily married. But I feel you."

I glance over my shoulder to watch her work. "You know what I wish?"

"What?"

"I wish men came with warning labels. You meet a guy who eyes you a certain way, and a voiceover explains what you'd really have to deal with after you hooked up with him."

The tingling under my skin intensifies, spreading well beyond the area she's tattooing. I grow dizzy. "Amelia, can I sit up for a second?"

"Sure. Take a minute. You want a cup of water?"

"Yes, please."

I shimmy my legs over the side of the chair and catch my breath. The guy catty-corner across from me waggles his eyebrows at me.

A booming male voice says, "While he prefers one-night-stands, no previous partners will testify he has the skill set to make the single evening count. Also known to make his conquests pay his tab."

I shake my head, an action not advisable for a person whose dizziness is causing hallucinations. My eyes dart around the room, landing on each of the male clients and tattoo artists for a split second, too short to even see their faces. I hope I'll find somebody holding a mic and in the process of pranking me. Man after man makes eye contact with me, but none speaks while looking at me. It makes no sense, though, because a chaotic soundtrack of phrases fills the air, spoken in the same announcer voice. The chatter is so layered, I can barely pick out more than a few random words.

"Married, but he's open to a little something on the side."

"He will forget your name but not your bra size."

"He is honest, funnier than most, and values inner beauty."

"Seeking back door priv…"

Wait. What was that previous statement I heard? Better yet, was that an actual description of a man nearby?

CHAPTER 6
GRIFFIN

I'm mildly surprised I've made it this far in life without a tattoo. Since I was a kid from the suburbs of New Jersey who thought he was cool to graduate from Green Day to bands like The Dillinger Escape Plan, I should have been deep in the tats years ago. But because I took my creative writing studies seriously, I didn't go through a rebellious phase. Plus, my sister commandeered my style decisions while I was her assistant. Under her guidance my curly, brownish hair gained a bit of height atop my long, narrow head; I adopted a pair of round tortoiseshell glasses; and I wore thin cashmere sweaters in bright colors over button-down shirts with the sleeves pushed up to my elbows. A tattoo would have been out of place for the West Coast version of the boy-next-door she had cultivated.

I'm free from Daphne's influence now, although the hairstyle and glasses she had chosen for me remain. Why it has taken five years to get myself into a chair at a tattoo gallery, I can't say, but sitting here in the basement of Inklyn under the gun of an overly bearded dude named Curly feels right.

"No one's ever asked me for abstract art before," he says.

"What designs do you typically ink?"

"Lots of skulls, howling wolves… I dig doing big pieces on people's backs of, say, a sunset in the background and a snake curling around a motorcycle."

"My design's too simple for you, isn't it?"

"Nah. I put the same effort into every tattoo. Have to make it clean and balanced. And I always enjoy inking with purpose. Some folks, when they ask me to tattoo around scars on their wrists, well, their scars represent hard times. Yours look more like an accident."

"Yup. It'd be cool to have a badass story to go along with them, but the truth is I burned myself making popcorn on the stove while drunk. The oil caught fire, and stupid me, I noticed the smoke, not the flames. Shouldn't have lifted the lid."

"Also got your face, I suppose."

I run my finger from the outer edge of my left eye to the corner of my mouth, following the puckered scar that tugs my eyelid nearly shut and renders the left side of my mouth in a permanent smile. "Yeah, I leaned over the pot to investigate. Poster child for poor decision making under the influence."

"And they couldn't fix the scar on your face?"

I grimace. I'm the master of tossing off a casual response to the first level of scar-related questions, but when people point out that I look like crap, well, one day, I'll find the courage to tell them what they can do with their questions.

"It was a second-degree burn. We couldn't guess how it would heal, but a graft was always more of a cosmetic option. Yeah, whatever."

"You're a good-looking guy. The right side of your face kind of reminds me of a movie star. How do the ladies deal with your, um…?"

I clench my left fist. *Shut up already and finish the damned tattoo, will you?*

I inhale slowly. "I prefer to believe it does me a favor by weeding out the shallow women. Anyone who sticks around is worthwhile."

"You found such a woman?"

"Not yet."

Curly hunches over my arm, inking the last blob of black before tackling the red streak. "You think you'd have better luck with a dating app?"

I see we've progressed to the stage of offering advice to the freak as if he's never considered his options.

"Which picture would I post? I choose a shot of the scar, and they swipe in the wrong direction. I hide it, and they're pissed when they discover I've deceived them. Best-case scenario for me is to fall into a relationship after I've become friends with a woman. I could use a good, old-fashioned pen pal."

Curly pulls the gun from my arm and glances at the ceiling. "I had a buddy when I was eight or nine. Never met him. Our class made friends with students in China. Jié and I stayed in touch for a year. I could tell him things I didn't tell my real-life friends."

"I hear you. Maybe it would be easier for me to open up in writing than in person."

It won't be, but Curly doesn't need the cold, hard facts. I'm only comfortable with the one-way street of writing fiction. Even messaging women, sight unseen, activates my self-consciousness to extreme levels. I had counted it a win for a man to check me in for my appointment instead of the woman who had called to confirm it. But it would be nice to be the kind of guy who can engage effortlessly with women.

I nod at Curly, who returns to his work on my arm. "Forget the dating apps. I wish that, for a reason totally unrelated to romance, I had to correspond with a woman before meeting her. We'd grow close, forge such a strong bond, even my face couldn't ruin the connection once we finally met in person."

I'm sure I'm imagining it, but a flow of warmth sweeps from my right forearm into my torso, up my neck, and behind my face, like the ink has seeped into my bloodstream. I let my body sink into the fake leather chair, enjoying the buzz.

Curly says, "Sure. Who's your dream chick? I'm married, which is not to say I don't, well, make friends outside my marriage. Don't know whether you've noticed the chick across from you, the girl whose tattoo artist stole your black ink. She's earned a starring role in my next fantasy."

I lift my head. A woman sits with her legs dangling over the side of her chair. Her skin is incandescent. Soft waves of pale blond hair cascade over her shoulder. Her eyes meet mine for a second before they dart around the room. "Yeah, I wouldn't stand a chance with her if we met in person. But it doesn't keep me from dreaming."

What keeps me from dreaming is how unlikely it would be for the woman across from me to see me beyond my scar. I can't raise my expectations every time my heart revs faster and my palms sweat upon falling for a woman at first sight. To believe anything beyond the truth would doom me to a repeated cycle of hope followed by heartache.

CHAPTER 7
ANJA

The voiceovers I had imagined quiet before Amelia returns with a cup of water. "Thanks," I say. "Don't take my spell personally. You have a gentle touch."

"I'm not offended. You ready for round two?"

I chug the water. "Let 'er rip."

"Once we make it through the outlines, the rest will be fun. Good thing I found my bottle of black, because this ink covers thoroughly on the first pass. It would take twice as long with a different ink."

"What makes your ink different?"

"I'm sure I sound crazy, but I swear it has a kind of intelligence where it knows how to interact with skin. Some inks are skittish, and you have to pump tons of it under the skin to make sure the color isn't patchy. Mystic Mate hangs out where I put it. Wish I could buy another bottle— someone sent my boss a sample last month—but it's not for sale. Saff is the coolest for bequeathing it to me."

"Thanks for choosing to sacrifice your stash for me."

"You deserve it. Curly's client? Who knows? At least he doesn't need a lot."

I twist my neck to get a glimpse of the guy in the chair across from me. Curly's broad back blocks my view of the man's face. The clients on either side of him meet my eyes while I survey the room. Each man grins in the same off-putting way they had while I thought I was hearing voices. Thankfully, the sound system and whirring tattoo machines drown out the conversations taking place elsewhere in the room. I'd hate to hear what anyone is thinking when they look at me.

And that's the dark side of my silly thought. Would I want to know everything about a guy up front? I've had decent experiences with men before things soured between us. Had I been aware of their faults from the start, I probably would have rejected them. Yeah, too much information at the beginning would make me gun-shy, and I'd wind up permanently single.

I should take Violet's advice and leave love to chance. The right guy will appear with or without my help. My job, my friends, and my volunteer gig keep me fulfilled. Better I enjoy the best my life offers rather than miss out on it because of my obsession with men.

Amelia sets her gun on her tray, her eyes looking spooked. "Oh, shoot!"

"Um, am I going to be mad at you?" I ask.

"Sorry, no. Your tattoo is perfect. I have to talk to Curly before his client leaves. The black ink comes with unusual care instructions. Give me a second."

The chair across from me is empty, and Curly is cleaning his station. Amelia flies up the spiral staircase. I bend my knee, drawing my ankle closer to my butt. The outline of the butterfly is complete. I'd call the tattoo done were it not for the fact the peacock-blue ink I chose has me friggin' jazzed. The edges of the outline are mind-blowingly clean. And there is a surprising absence of gore. I'm not saying I wanted her to tear my leg into a bloody, pulpy mess, but it's what I had expected.

The threat of pain had scared me, but truthfully, I've discovered the biggest turnoff of getting a tattoo is the boredom. And sitting in the middle of a sea of men, I'm feeling a tad exposed. I drum my fingers on the chair, keeping my eyes pointed above the heads of everyone and pretending I'm alone.

Amelia returns, breathless. "Sorry for abandoning you. If the ink didn't behave uniquely, I'd have tossed the aftercare instructions the first time I read them. They're not just weird; they also rhyme. Anyhow, instead of removing the bandage tomorrow, keep the tattoo out of the light for a week. Here, read the instructions for yourself."

She hands me a piece of paper folded into thirds lengthwise and then across. I push the edges with my thumbs to open it. "Sheesh, this is worse than the poetry I wrote in third grade."

> *Never shall I see the sun until one hundred sixty-eight hours are done. Let me hide beneath my cover so I can shine when the week is over.*

Amelia takes the paper from me and places it on her metal tray before loading her gun with the darker blue ink. "I know, right? But I wouldn't fool with it. The ink could be unstable for the first week. No harm in being cautious in order to protect the intensity of the color. Clean the tattoo in a dimly lit room after sundown."

"Or what: I turn into a vampire? My friend Violet wore a bandage over hers for a few days. I'll ask her how she feels about garlic and wooden stakes."

"Violet with the violets on her arm?"

"Yup. You tattooed her, right?"

"Sure did. With the same ink as you. How does it look?"

"It's stunning. I love it, and your work is flawless."

She shrugs, grinning confidently. "I told you, I'm a pro. What I meant was, is the black as deep and inky as yours?"

"Like the paint's still wet."

"Cool. Her tattoo proves the ink and the care instruction's thirteen-year-old boy's fantasy vibe should be taken seriously. Anyhow, let's take care of you. The next part is fun. I'll pack the darker blue on the upper ends and pepper it down to blend into the lighter shade. Same with the green. The interior of the wings will go much faster than the black borders. You ready?"

"Yes, ma'am." I pull my phone from my pocket to check in with my resident tattoo expert.

> **Anja:** I joined your tattoo club.

> **Violet:** Awesome. Can't wait to see it.

> **Anja:** Gotta wait a week. Like you did.

Three dots appear, recede, and reappear. I exit the message app, prepared to put away my phone rather than wait for her to respond. My phone blurps at me before I put it in my pocket.

> **Violet:** Did they use Mystic Mate ink?

> **Anja:** That they did. We're tattoo twins.

> **Violet:** Call me later. It's important. And whatever you do, DON'T TAKE OFF THE BANDAGE!

I scoff. Violet can be a bit dramatic.

> **Anja:** Trust me, will you?

Despite my response, my body buzzes with a warning. I shove my phone into my pocket and try to do the same with my building sense of dread.

31

CHAPTER 8
GRIFFIN

"No, seriously. Ridunculous as the poem is, you need to follow the directions to the letter." The tiny, breathless woman with pink hair who was tattooing the goddess across from me downstairs shoves three bandages into my hand. "The ink Curly used— or should I say stole from me—behaves differently. I'd hate for you to lose the depth of its color. Keep that puppy out of the light every second of the next week, and I promise you your tattoo will be the envy of all your friends once it has healed."

The word healed captures my imagination. I've always wondered whether my scars would have been less prominent had I gone to the hospital the night I set fire to my face and kitchen. Stupid, drunk Griffin waited until things became decidedly more painful and slimier the next day before seeking medical help.

"Thanks for the warning."

I pat the black bandage stretched over the inside of my forearm. Since I'm not a shout-it-from-the-rooftop kind of guy, hiding the bandage under a long-sleeved shirt while I'm in LA is fine by me. The less interesting I am to Daphne, the better.

Inklyn is a mile walk from my Hamilton Park apartment. The elevated New Jersey Turnpike and the approach to the Holland Tunnel frame two sides of my quiet neighborhood. Drivers stuck in traffic are none the wiser to the slower-paced world below the roadways.

Every once in a while, I have a hankering to adopt a dog. Between the fact that I work from home and love taking walks on my breaks, a dog could do worse than share my second-floor apartment with me. After five years in the neighborhood, I'm more familiar with the exterior of the homes than their occupants. A dog would change everything. It would attract people to us.

On the last block of 7th Street before I turn onto my street, nearly identical row houses line each side. Save for variations in the color of the brick or the style of railings, one building blends into the next. Even the window treatments adhere to the dictum of monotony. The curtains or shades are always white. They hang with choreographed precision. Except for the unit on the second floor of the middle building on the north side.

Each of the four windows sports curtains—or more likely, scraps of fabric—in different colors and levels of opaqueness. None hang to the same height or run parallel to the windowsills. The left window's gold fabric covers the most square footage and lets the least amount of light through it. A diaphanous billow of fringed purple cloth flutters in front of window number three, which is open. Boxes filled with plants and what appear to be plastic toys hang below each window. You can't help but wonder about who lives inside.

I stare at the facade, twisting the details of the home in my mind to suit my current work-in-progress. Talib, a nineteen-year-old who, in the first book of the series, had escaped enslavement on a plantation in Louisiana, will meet a love interest soon. He travels west in a six-legged vehicle he designed. Perhaps I'll have him pass through a small community where he meets an adventurer whose imagination rivals his but whose style provides a contrast. He abides by the laws of physics to build his vehicles and automatons. She is a free spirit untethered to conventional ideas. Together, they can conquer the world, or at least their dreams.

Yeah, whatever. I'll make a note to address the plot idea later. First, I need to conquer the coming week. I turn onto my street, dragging my feet.

My pace slows for another reason. Inexplicably, I tug my phone from my back pocket and reread Mallory's text. Before I can control my fingers, they type and send a response.

> **Griffin:** It's been so long since we've been in touch, we might officially be strangers. Which begs the question, didn't your mother warn you not to talk to strangers? Now you're stuck reading a text from some random man.

My words don't sound like mine. Well, they don't resemble anything I would type or say to any woman besides my sister. Whoever this stranger inside me is, I must rescind his phone privileges before he sends the wrong message to my ex.

TUESDAY

CHAPTER 9
ANJA

I am itching to remove my bandage. Not that I'm experiencing any such symptoms at the site of the tattoo. I hardly remember the encounter my ankle had with thousands upon thousands of needle pricks last night. My nail digs under a corner of a piece of tape. Who in their right mind would expect someone who picked every scab— of which there were many in her youth since it took her years to get the hang of owning larger-than-average feet— to keep her mitts off her brand-new tattoo and keep it hidden from sight?

I should hire Violet to save me from myself. Oh, crap. Violet. I have to check in with her even though I should leave for work in less than ten minutes. She'll kill me for forgetting to call her last night. I pull my phone from my purse.

> **Anja:** Babe, sorry I didn't call you last night. One thing led to another. You know.

Violet: I've learned to temper my expectations with you. Except on matters pertaining to your tattoo. Please promise me you haven't peeked at it.

Anja: Almost, but my angel-on my-shoulder (who, BTW, bears a striking resemblance to you) smacked me upside my head before I did.

Violet: You keep listening to your angel. She knows of what she speaks. I only have a second, but I need you to answer a question. Are you, oh, this is going to sound weird… Are you still you?

Anja: Like, der. Who else would I be?

Violet: I'll explain one day. Anything strange happen while you got the tattoo?

I can't determine whether hearing an announcer describe the characteristics of half a dozen men counts as peculiar. Sure, it would have been strange had it been real, but I blame a hungry tummy, a sore ankle, and an active imagination for making me believe I was hearing voices.

Anja: All good.

Violet: So, you didn't make any wishes last night?

Anja: Wishes? Do you mean did a wish I made come true? I can't decide whether you or Tracey should win the prize for least likely to believe in magic. Doesn't matter. If anyone isn't being her true self, it's you.

Violet: I might surprise you. Anyway, I have to run. I'd never hear the end of it were I the person to make Ben and me late for work. Chat later. Oh, and don't you dare remove your bandage!

I'm tempted to remove it simply to mess with Violet. She's lucky her tattoo is freaking gorgeous. I want my black ink to pop the way hers does. Fine. I'll follow the directions.

The clock says I should have left a minute ago, but it has been a while since I watered my outdoor plants, and today is going to be sunny. Can't let the poor things die of dehydration.

I heave the farthest window in my living room upward with my shoulder, both of us groaning from the effort.

"Jerome, you were supposed to alert me when the plants needed watering," I say to the Lego dinosaur who threatens to munch my one remaining marigold. "I've never been able to trust Bert and Ernie, but you? I expected more. Guess this is why your peeps went extinct."

I douse the flower before moving on to the next window. My basil plant appears to be giving me the finger. A lone branch of green sprouts from a sea of shriveled, brown leaves in which a rubber ducky swims. Ernie has slipped from the popsicle stick I had inserted into his nether regions. Can't blame the dude for lying down on the job after the indignity I've forced on him. Bert stares at the street, nonplussed.

The cacti in box number three alone give me hope I will not face charges of herbicide. Giving credit where credit is due, I run my finger along the edge of the Día de Muertos mask wedged into the dirt. "Muchas gracias, mi amigo." I serenade the cacti with a chorus of *Besame Mucho* while giving the soil, which is dryer than the desert on Mars, a sprinkling of water.

At the end of the song, I slam the window shut and grab my purse. Can't be late—again—because I was talking to my garden. I bolt downstairs and hightail it to the light rail station over half a mile away. I keep my eyes on the sidewalk while I hustle for the train. I've learned skinned knees aren't just for kids. Easily distracted women are a favorite prey of uneven pavement. I can't take in more of my surroundings than my lavender Converse high tops until I reach the train platform.

Ooh! Handsome man alert at eight o'clock. He rubs his palm ever so seductively across stubbly brown hair, clenching a jaw worthy of a comic book hero while he reads a text. His eyes, a shade of blue not dissimilar to the darker color of my new butterfly friend, lift and meet mine. He smiles.

"This man offers little beyond his attractive features except for an active case of herpes."

I stagger backward and bump into the garbage can behind me. What the actual fudge is going on here?

CHAPTER 10
GRIFFIN

I stumble from my ride share onto the sidewalk in front of my sister's office in West Hollywood a few minutes before noon on Tuesday. The pre-dawn wake-up call and five-and-a-half-hour flight did nothing to alter the foul mood I packed along with my laptop.

The skin on my cheeks betrays me, happily drinking in the warmth of the Southern California sun. And this block, running perpendicular to Santa Monica Boulevard and Melrose, has lost little of its familiarity in the last five years. I could shut off my brain and pretend I belong here, but what fun would that be? I kick my roller bag upright and wheel it toward the middle of the three doors in the white stucco, two-story building.

With a fortifying breath, I pull the door's handle and enter. The office resembles a fire sale. Dark brown and white speckled cardboard file boxes outnumber both the people and the furniture inside. The chaos would scare away a new client. Good thing they aren't accepting any.

In the eighties, K. C. Adams inherited the firm her father had founded forty years earlier. While she and her assistant publicists will go to hell and back for their clients, their business model is archaic compared to their competitors who came of age during the advent of social media. Better the firm close upon K. C.'s retirement than to reinvent itself.

Daphne had received three job offers before she even considered finding a new position. Unlike me, change invigorates her. I brace myself, creating a force field against whatever energetic cheerfulness she's readying for me. I tuck my suitcase behind a potted rubber tree in the front window and scan the room.

"Griffin!" Daphne drops a Manila file folder on a desk and rushes to greet me. "You told me you would call after you landed."

"We're still circling above LAX. I'll text you when we're wheels down."

"Smart ass. Can I put you straight to work?"

"Sure. I have an idea. Can I haul the boxes of dead files to your house and deal with them there?"

"I haven't seen you in seven months. I need to have you brooding in a corner of the office to make our visit complete. Follow me. I've cleared a spot for you."

I tug the cuff of my right sleeve to shift the opening at the placket away from her prying eyes. It would be easier to hide my bandage under a long-sleeved T-shirt, but then she'd hassle me for not wearing a collared shirt. With my eyes facing the floor, I shuffle past two unfamiliar assistants, stopping in my tracks in front of the boss.

"Call the press! Griffin Hull spotted in West Hollywood." K. C. swoops in for a hug. "Honey, we've missed you."

Some describe the boss as a battle-axe. Her helmet of straw-yellow hair and too-large, red-framed glasses haven't changed in the last thirty years, even if she has shrunk beneath them. She can open any metaphorical door and will shove someone aside to clear a path if needed. Her whiskey voice causes half the men in town to shiver in their Gucci loafers. But to me, she's the grandmother of my dreams.

I wrap my arms around her bony shoulders. "I should have visited sooner. Congrats on your retirement."

"Don't know what I'm going to do with myself, but the time is right for me to step aside and let the younger generation rule the world."

"I doubt Hollywood has seen the last of you."

"I'm ready for my exit, honey."

Daphne sets a file box on an otherwise empty desk with a bang, eager to capture my attention. I kiss K. C. on her cheek and claim my workspace.

"I have a bone to pick with you," I say to my sister.

"Don't you always?"

"You might want to consider why you generally put me in a mood. To make things easier for you, I'll clue you in on why I'm mad at you today. What part of telling nobody I was in town did you not understand? I nearly tore up the plane ticket after Mallory texted me yesterday."

Daphne claps her hands, delighted to hear my ex's name. "She contacted you! Awesome!"

"No, not awesome. Are you really this thick?"

"I must be."

"She tore out my heart and stomped on it. Why on earth would I jump for joy at the chance to reconnect with her during my visit? Sheesh, Daphne! Could you be more obtuse?"

"I don't carry your prejudices. I remember her being kind, compassionate, and capable of bringing out your best side."

So do I, Daphne. So do I.

"She and I ran into each other in line at a local juice bar yesterday. She's pursuing a new career path. I'll let her explain. But you're both older and wiser. Wouldn't you love the chance to replace the villain you've cast her as with a version more in line with the person you know her to be?"

"Honestly, I was perfectly content not thinking about her at all."

Which is, of course, a total lie.

CHAPTER 11
ANJA

"Ah, shoot! I forgot to bring my guitar with me today." I slam my hand against my desk.

"Are you referring to the guitar you left in the coat closet on Friday?" Alejandro, my colleague, asks.

I run to the closet and remove the beat-up black guitar case. "Man, I'm two for two. I brought it on Friday to take to my volunteer gig, but they canceled on me before I left the office. Makes sense that I forgot to take it home. At least it solves the problem of me being the world's most absent-minded person."

"This time." Alejandro embellishes the punch line with a grin.

I wrinkle my nose. "I don't need to take any guff from you."

He's not wrong to remind me I've solved but one problem and am bound to create another before long, but I don't have it in me to endure a gentle ribbing. My nerves have already met their jangle quota for the day.

After my introduction to Herpes Man on the train platform earlier, I heard three more voiceovers during my commute. Each described a man less savory than the last. Coming on the heels of last night's announcer fest and Violet's odd texts, I had to conclude it might be more than my imagination at play.

On the train, I jotted my observations into a notebook I found at the bottom of my purse, starting with mentioning my desire to possess a certain superpower first to my best friends and then during my tattoo appointment. It couldn't be a coincidence to have a disembodied voice follow me around, could it? I noted the announcer's statements have used male pronouns to describe people, which means I'm safe from learning the secrets of random women. Question #1: Did I hear voices after I made eye contact with men? Question #2: Did I hear descriptions about the men with whom I made eye contact? Question #3: What is happening to me?

I transcribed the individual descriptions the best I could remember. The list I compiled described a rogues' gallery of cheaters, rump raiders, and bedpost notchers. Except for one. Who was the funny, honest guy who finds hidden beauty?

I suppose I might never know. The best I can hope for is the voice to guide me to him or someone equally engaging, but the voice has stopped narrating. True, since I haven't stepped foot outside the office in hours, I haven't had contact with any men besides Alejandro. He doesn't seem to merit an introduction. I figure I can blame the radio silence on either his lack of interest in dating me or that we have previously met.

Having a theory gives me a modicum of comfort. On my way to the care facility, my intention is to hear nothing besides the usual rush hour noise. I must look suspicious AF, shifting my eyes downward whenever I approach another person coming toward me. It's worth it, though, because I make it to my destination with nary a verbal distraction.

Sheltered within the vestibule of the facility, my shoulders peel away from my ears. Odds of meeting an eligible man for the first time here are slim. A few of the male residents have never been shy about voicing their desires. I appreciate the honesty. Young men could learn a lot from their elders.

"¡Hola, chica!" Maria waves to me from behind the reception desk. "Everybody's waiting for you in the dining room."

"It's not five-thirty yet, is it?"

"You have five minutes. Doesn't matter. Cocktail hour with Anja is more popular than Bingo. People were in their seats an hour ago."

"How early would they arrive if we offered them real cocktails?"

"Ay, no booze for the residents. We'd lose control." Her hands flutter aside her head. "Better get moving before you're late."

"Wouldn't be the first time."

I hustle into the dining room and lay my guitar case across the arms of a chair positioned to face the audience. A woman taps me on my back. I spin around, jittery from the unexpected touch.

"Oh, Mrs. Perlmutter, you startled me."

"When does the show go on?"

"At five-thirty, like usual."

"Are they giving us nuts? I can't eat nuts."

"I'm the only nut around here. For you and everyone else, there will be crackers and lemonade before they serve dinner. What should I play first?"

I tune my guitar while she taps her fingertips together and bounces her head with her eyes cast heavenward. The process of selecting a tune requires much deliberation, but the answer never varies.

"*Mairzy Doats*. Do you know it?"

"You picked my favorite. Have a seat, and I'll play it for you."

I spend forty hours a week tending to the impressive careers of some of the world's finest classical musicians. I write their program biographies and publicity materials while my boss and Alejandro determine what recital venues to book for an artist's nationwide tour or who should make her Metropolitan Opera debut in what role. None of our artists need to hear me belt nursery rhymes while accompanying myself on the guitar. They can have their Carnegie Hall audiences; I'll take my senior peeps any day of the week.

"Hello, Cincinnati!" I say once my guitar is in tune.

"This isn't Ohio. You must have gotten off at the wrong exit," Mrs. Ellis says.

I rise from my chair with a start. "My bad. Excuse me, I need to find my gig."

"You're in the right place, sweetheart. Enough tomfoolery. Play us a tune, would ya?"

"Right away, sir. Here's an old chestnut you might remember from back in the day."

I pluck a knotty, chromatic chord of random notes.

"Boo! What's that nonsense you're playing?"

"Rude, Mr. Cohn. Rude. I spent at least six seconds composing my masterpiece. Here. I'll play it again. Familiarity is the secret to learning to love new music."

I add a layer of vocal screeching to my intro. The room erupts in laughter. Well, except for Mr. Lowenstein. He stares at his lap, as usual. The aids won't serve him crackers or dinner, either, on account of his feeding tube. Every week, they roll him into the room, hoping something will reach him. I haven't abandoned hope yet that my music could be the magic potion.

I collect the notes spewing from my fingertips, shifting from random patterns into a simple, quarter note strum on a G major chord. "Oh... Mairzy doats and..."

After a rousing chorus or three, we move on to *Bye, Bye Blackbird* and *My Old Kentucky Home*.

"Okay, folks, next up is me potentially falling flat on my face. You promise to be kind?"

"No. Play it anyway," Mr. Cohn says.

I'm a strumming kind of gal, but a recital by a guitarist on our roster at The Shed a couple of weeks ago inspired me to up my game and learn to pluck a melody above an accompaniment. My fingers have the grace and coordination of The Three Stooges, but I've convinced them they can handle a simplified version of *El Choclo*.

I establish a stolid tango groove before diving into the melody above it. The challenge of plucking individual strings pulls my head toward my instrument, forcing me to stare at my fingers rather than connect to my audience. From the corner of my eye, I catch sight of unexpected movement. I'm too curious to ignore it. I insert an elongated interlude of repeated measures of the basic tango rhythm between verses, which allows me to lessen my concentration and lift my head.

Mr. Lowenstein has done the same. He has his left hand palm up on the armrest of his wheelchair, and his fingers make small, quivering movements in time with the music, like a beetle marooned on his back but enjoying the tunes. Mr. Lowenstein's eyes meet mine.

The booming announcer dude's voice drowns out my guitar. "This man had forgotten who he was, but now he remembers."

CHAPTER 12
GRIFFIN

The two boxes waiting for me in my corner contain photos, press clippings, and correspondences related to four artists. Three are actors whose names would draw a blank from even a self-proclaimed expert on the Golden Age of Hollywood. Bit parts in forgotten movies define their careers. Can't wager a guess why they hired a publicist, but thanks to bursts of optimism, they signed with Jerome Adams in the late forties. A quick trip to Wikipedia reveals none of the actors are alive today.

I ball my fists, frustration slithering within my chest and shoulders. Their grandchildren must already have more mementos from Granny or Gramp's glamorous career than they have storage space. Who would want to add another foot of material to their attic?

"Daphne, I don't see the point of unloading the files on unsuspecting heirs. I bet everything in here is a duplicate. Why are you wasting my time, making me hunt down relatives to send them a few scraps of paper? If you dragged me to LA under false pretenses, we have a serious problem."

"I promise you, our intentions are solid. The files represent a comprehensive documentation of our clients' careers, and their families will treasure the new troves of material. Don't flake out on me by being lazy."

"Work doesn't scare me. Pointless work and ulterior motives will piss me off, though."

"Yeah, yeah, yeah. More research, less whining."

I place three stacks of files at the back of my desk, making more noise in the process than the task merits. The remaining paperwork in the box belongs to a classical music duo, Canaro y Roca. A folder opens to a photo of a woman whose hair is jet black save for a dramatic silver streak skirting the edge of her face. She bends forward, squeezing an accordion-like instrument at her waist. Her companion grips a violin under his chin and holds his bow aloft. His dark hair flounces away from his head like a dancer's skirt, mid-spin. The action shot is an antidote to the actors' fake grins in their publicity photos. It hooks me into my assigned project.

I sort the duo's materials into piles at the front of my desk, setting the photos on the left, newspaper clippings in the middle, and the letters and copies of bills on the right. The oldest correspondences place the start of their relationship with J. Adams Publicity in 1955. The most recent bill dates from 1973, nearly fifty years ago.

Two years spent assisting my sister taught me the publicity firm isn't interested in family members unless they're photogenic (babies; famous spouses) or liabilities (see also: babies; famous spouses). The chances of unearthing useful information about next-of-kin in any of the files are no better than the odds of me opting to spend an afternoon lounging at the Tropicana Pool at The Hollywood Roosevelt.

I scan a lengthy 1962 piece from the LA Times, written prior to an appearance at Royce Hall at UCLA. It includes several quotes from Arminda Canaro, the pianist and bandoneon player. She spoke on behalf of León Roca, the violinist. The two formed the duo ten years prior to the concert. Originally dedicated to presenting classical repertoire, they began slipping pieces from their native Argentina into their programs. From a publicist's perspective, the changeover to the nuevo tango, a blend of tango, classical, and jazz, was money.

The duo's album, *Nunca oprimida* from 1970, appears at the top of the search list YouTube shows me when I type in their name. I hit play.

Lacking live footage, the video displays a black-and-white photo of the musicians, whose energy borders on maniacal, while the music plays. The bandoneon utters a plaintive motif, repeating it an octave higher and evoking a café in Buenos Aires on a warm afternoon. After the violin's sweet and playful entrance, the bandoneon chases it rather than ropes it into a steady beat. It's beautiful, but it leaves me wanting to hear more of the pair's passion within the notes. I fast forward to the second track.

The violin and bandoneon sing a frantic tune in unison while Canaro also mashes out a jazzy, messy tango rhythm on her instrument. The recording is the sonic equivalent of eating an overly ripe peach with no concern for preventing the sticky juice from dribbling on your face.

"Keep it down, would you? I'm on a call," Daphne says to me over her shoulder.

I pause the video and mouth my apologies. Finding Canaro y Roca almost seems worth my trip west.

The phone number printed on the stationery Ms. Canaro used during her early correspondences with J. Adams Publicity is laughably antiquated. MOnument 5-5551. I dig further and land on a letter from Apollo Artists, their management firm in New York City.

I search for them online. An arts management company of the same name appears. I click on their website, which is the opposite of the vibe expressed by MOnument 5-5551. The home page is full of white space and well-chosen fonts. The company represents an impressive roster of established musicians even I've heard of. Go figure: Canaro y Roca is not on their list.

I fill out the contact form with my query. I'm not banking on receiving a helpful response—and certainly not today, given the time difference, but it seems like a good starting point. And an even better finishing point. My body thinks it's six-thirty—cocktail hour. Who am I to deny it beer and chips?

CHAPTER 13
ANJA

I break into a sweat. Too freaked out to handle the challenges of returning to the tune and too stressed by the burden of maintaining my connection with Mr. Lowenstein, I comp another four bars before diving into the next verse. He stays with me until the end of the song.

What had I done to yank him from his fog? I desperately want to recapture the magic. His left hand had twitched along with mine. Could he have, in his youth, learned to play *El Choclo* on the guitar?

I have nothing else in my repertoire a classical guitarist would play. Despite no legit training in music therapy, I've heard that when a key, tempo, or rhythm elicits a reaction from a patient, you should stick with it. I wrack my brain for a Latin tune in d minor, the same key as *El Choclo*. Ah, *Besame Mucho* will do.

It's a favorite with this crowd, and they respond happily to the opening lyrics interspersed with smooching sounds. Mr. Lowenstein's hand slips into his lap, and his head droops toward his chest. He's gone.

My heart also loses interest in the program. Aides slide dinner trays in front of the residents, and by six-fifteen, it is time to call it quits. I sling my guitar over my shoulder and approach Mr. Lowenstein.

"I'm glad you enjoyed *El Choclo*. May I play an encore for you?"

He doesn't raise his head. I drag a chair next to him and lightly pluck the tune for him. Again, his fingers move with mine. Blood pumps within my chest as fast as my sixteenth notes. I catch the eye of an aide and gesture with my head toward Mr. Lowenstein. She hurries to his side.

"Well, Mr. Lowenstein. You are full of pep today. You like Miss Anja's music?"

His eyes don't stray from the fingerboard of my guitar. I hold my breath, hoping not to break the spell.

"You must be playing his favorite song, my dear. In the year that I've worked here, I've never seen him respond to anything."

I switch to the simple tango accompaniment pattern, freeing my brain to handle both the music and a conversation. "Is he verbal?"

"No."

"Did he play guitar?"

"He's a mystery. I believe he lost his wife a few years ago. He never has visitors. He lives inside his mind. But he connects to you, see?"

I resume the melody. Mr. Lowenstein has closed his eyes, and his head sways side to side in time with the music. While not exactly smiling, he has stopped mashing his lips together in his signature jumpy frown. I feel more powerful for reaching him than for any other ability I possess, including being able to hear my stupid announcer friend tell me the dirt on eligible men.

CHAPTER 14
GRIFFIN

"Glad to see you don't hate everyone in LA," Daphne says, lowering herself into the lounger next to me on her back patio.

Charlotte and Liam, her children, busy themselves with a collection of brightly colored plastic vehicles, which they navigate around the obstacle course of furniture.

"They're easy to love because they didn't betray their uncle. And they inherited my palate. We enjoyed a feast of chicken nuggets for dinner."

"Sorry to force you to scrounge in the freezer for your dinner, but I'm glad you and the kids ate. I didn't expect to be home so late, and Brad won't be home for a while still. You want another beer?"

I hand her my empty can. "Don't mind if I do."

"Let's move the party inside. I'm starving."

I commandeer an abandoned blue dump truck. "Crew, the boss called and said it's time to pack it in. He's paying bonuses to the first two members of the team to return to the kitchen. As your supervisor, it behooves me to set a good example. I'm heading in. Doesn't make sense for me to miss out on a bonus, does it?"

Liam bashes his tractor into the rear of my truck. "What does behoose mean?"

"Behoove, like beehive with an *ooh*. It means grownups should take responsibility for their actions. Last truck driver inside has to watch the winners devour their ice cream sandwiches."

"No fair! Ice cream sandwiches are for kids, not grownups."

"Then you'd better hustle, buddy!"

Liam scoops his truck under his arm and races through the open sliding glass door. Charlotte squats to pick up a pebble to add to the collection in the bucket of her backhoe.

"Char, I admire your work ethic. Nobody removes pebbles from the grooves between pavers with your dedication. But there's an ice cream sandwich with your name on it inside. If you don't eat it, I will. Afterwards, I'll tickle you."

She giggles and buckles, protecting her belly from my roving fingers. "No tickles!" She runs away from me fast enough to put the Doppler effect to good use on the last syllable of her sentence.

Daphne pushes herself to a standing position. "I suppose someone tall enough to reach into the freezer should be in the kitchen before they call their union rep."

"Let me. I'm running in to grab the beer you offered but never procured. But then I might return to my lounger. I have to be in touch with a couple of people."

"Mallory?" Her elbow plants itself below my ribcage.

Her question doesn't merit a response. I shove past her to dole out ice cream and beer to the deserving.

The chaos level of hungry mothers and sugar-addicted kids provides cover for me to slip onto the patio with a can of a local brewery's hazy IPA. I can't discount the pleasure of drinking a brew not available on the East Coast in a quiet backyard. Perhaps escaping Jersey City for a few days isn't the worst thing.

And along those lines, perhaps texting Mallory again wouldn't be a terrible idea, in case she didn't receive my first message. Again, I find my impulse to initiate a conversation with her to be inexplicable. I type a quick message and hit send before I can chicken out.

> **Griffin:** Based on your silence, I must commend you on refusing to talk to strangers. Unlike yesterday, since I'm in your time zone, you can't use the excuse of not wanting to keep a guy on EDT awake with the endless buzz of message notifications.

> **Mallory:** I knew you were a traitor the second we met. Your area code might still belong to LA, but that heart of yours never left NJ.

I stare at my phone, unnerved by my easy tone and to have heard from her right away. Somehow, the part about her returning my text had never crossed my mind. She doesn't give me time to regroup, instead sending another message seconds later.

> **Mallory:** Can you find a moment in your busy schedule to meet for drinks?

> **Griffin:** Might not happen. Sorry.

> **Mallory:** You're leaving my imagination to conjure the reason the great Griffin Hull is too busy for an old friend.

> **Griffin:** Everything you've landed on is true.

> **Mallory:** I knew it. You're CIA, right?

> **Griffin:** To say more would put your life at risk.

Mallory: Ah, that is where you are wrong, my friend. I have come to the US to hunt you down.

Griffin: Should I call you Natasha?

Mallory: Why?

Griffin: You're working for the Russians.

Mallory: No, not the Russians. The Andorrans.

Griffin: Shoot. I always worried my adventure with the flock of sheep and the ski lift would catch up to me.

Mallory: They have skiing in Andorra?

Griffin: I see the spying game is new for you. Pro tip: visit a country before you do their dirty work. And trust me: cleaning up after a dozen sheep have gone airborne is the dirtiest job around.

Mallory: This is nice.

Griffin: What, reading my discourses on the scatological pitfalls of tending sheep in a ski resort?

Mallory: Connecting. Chatting with you is easy. I haven't had a lot of easy in my life lately.

My fingers skid to a halt. Until she mentioned it, the flow between us had prevented me from dwelling on who was on the other end. Easy is the right word for it. I had lost myself in our dialogue. Which is unusual, not simply because I'm texting with Mallory.

This is how she and I used to talk. I had enough swagger before my accident not to let my proximity to a major star the first night she and I met intimidate me. It took mere seconds to forget her fame once we were doubled over from laughter. The charm she oozed on screen was genuine. I lost myself in her when we were together. And I lost myself again after she dumped me.

It's freeing to text a woman who can't see my face. I should have learned to tame my defenses earlier. Having no end game with Mallory simplifies matters further.

A shiver creeps along my spine. I had imagined this very scenario—connecting to a woman via my phone—twenty-four hours ago. I never put any stakes in the significance of coincidences, yet having mentioned my wish to Curly during the tattoo appointment about connecting deeply with a woman out of the dating context and out of sight, I can't help but take note.

WEDNESDAY

CHAPTER 15
ANJA

Mrs. Cuthbert, my boss, is old school. She prefers handling paper to pixels, and judging from the state of my sagging inbox this morning, I bet she stayed late at the office last night, dreaming of busywork for me. I sort the projects she wants me to tackle today from easiest to manage before my second cup of coffee to things I wish would resolve themselves without my intervention.

Unfortunately, Wednesday is shorthand for "Monday's projects, which I had hoped I'd never confront again, have returned to bite me on the behind." She has left me a memo, reminding me the company's newsletter should have arrived at our mail fulfillment center yesterday. It's possible I might have forgotten to contact the printer on Monday to verify that he had shipped the order last Friday. I definitely want to relocate the message to my wait-until-later pile, but I'm guessing my boss wouldn't care to know I had shoved the project to the back burner a second time this week. I promise I will get to it before lunch.

My job performance isn't the most accurate reflection of my capabilities. This is my dream job. I earn my living by using my writing chops to promote classical musicians. I find it meaningful and fulfilling. Except when I don't.

Between Mrs. Cuthbert's efforts to single-handedly keep the local branch of the Post Office operational and her insistence I write our artists' biographical and publicity materials in the stilted voice of a World War II-era newsreel, I don't have the chance to put my stamp on my creations. It would be awesome for her to allow me to write pieces that reflect the way our younger musicians present themselves on social media. I'd also prefer to distribute them digitally. And if my boss trusted my vision, perhaps it would inspire me to take a more methodical approach to my job. But she dismisses my suggestions without fail. Which is why I turn to coffee for my morning motivation.

I loiter in the kitchen, stirring my coffee with seeming purpose while I wait for a distraction. I mentally clap my hands in response to the sound of footsteps approaching the kitchenette. "Oh, hey, Alejandro. I was heading to my desk, but I'll stay if you want company." I could not be more cazh.

He spins to let the fridge catch him mid-swoon. "Please stay. Can I tell you about my date last night?"

My plan worked to perfection.

"Yeah, I have a minute or two to spare. Are we looking at a 'book the caterer' or 'hire a hitman' situation?"

"The latter. You know anyone?"

"I'll put you in touch with my guy." I rapidly open and close several of the cabinets. "Coffee alone ain't gonna cut it for a date dissection. Do we have any more of the Danish butter cookies?"

"Long gone, honey. Freja Møller's Carnegie Hall recital was over a week ago."

"Still, she gifted us a tin of two hundred cookies. I couldn't have eaten more than…" I stare at my fingers, fluttering them in the air like Mr. Lowenstein's did during yesterday's performance. "Two hundred divided by eight is… Someone else had to have attacked them with more vigor than me. I'm sure I didn't exceed my fair share of twenty-five."

He jabs his thumb upward.

"Fine. Forty. But Bev is gluten free, Delia won't eat anything with a carbon footprint as large as a cookie made in Denmark, and Mrs. Cuthbert frowns upon interrupting important matters for petty activities such as eating. Which means my math still holds. What say you, Mr. I'd-Rather-Judge-You-Than-Admit-My-Guilt?"

"Weren't we talking about my date?"

"Uh, huh. Perhaps you carb loaded beforehand?"

"Please don't let my story interrupt your obsessive search for the missing cookies."

He totally bears responsibility for the untimely end to our cookie stash, but I'm too kind to point out the obvious. I wave my hands in front of my face, magically erasing my memory of cookies that, to be honest, weren't actually so delicious. "Cookies forgotten. Please, tell me about Mr. Wrong."

"I'm no longer in the mood. I swear, dating would be easier if men came with the equivalent of a nutritional label."

My head involuntarily jerks backwards. So many ideas swirl in my brain, I half expect my head to explode. But then I'd be stuck cleaning myself off the walls. Wasn't my trip to the kitchenette designed to avoid unwanted projects?

If we held hands and he posed his suggestion in the form of a wish, would my power transfer to him? I'd love to be free from my pesky announcer, but I wouldn't wish my condition on Alejandro.

Can I reveal my superpower to him? Would he believe me? Do I even believe I possess the ability to hear the worst about a man before entangling my life with his?

I scratch the back of my neck. "Sounds useful, but I could imagine it being overwhelming. What happens when you read a guy's label, which is pitch-perfect, on the day you're a total disaster? No way he's sharing his digits."

His eyes scan the length of me. I stand behind my choice of wearing a red gingham blouse and denim miniskirt, thank you very much. I didn't choose today's outfit with the intention of pleasing him.

He says, "I never leave the house in any state less than flawless. Well, except for today, thanks to my monster zit."

"You have a monster?"

He points to a patch of skin in the hollow between his cheekbone and jaw. I see only his perfectly buffed fingernail. "He adopted me, and I can't make him leave."

"I don't see anything."

"You can't see a tap-dancing pimple wearing a "Hello, My Name is Mr. Zit" badge and cavorting on my cheek?"

"Now, were it six feet tall and dancing in the middle of the office, he and I would already be best friends. But honestly, I don't see things like zits. Fun hats, yes. Animated body language, expressive eyes, that's what I notice. The little flaws someone hates about themself, those are the things I tend not to see. To me, you are always dazzling."

He holds his hands to his chest and closes his eyes. "Thank you, my dear, but nobody else has your generous eye. Because we live in a world ruled by judgmental people, my entire life philosophy revolves around being ready to dazzle at any moment."

That sounds as exhausting as it is to be single. My friend Tracey has teased me for being boy crazy since we were teens. I'd give anything to break my habit. With my newly installed soundtrack, I have to be on my game one hundred percent of the time while I'm in public. Remembering to keep my head lowered or else endure a barrage of unsavory descriptions about the hordes of men who seem desperate for me to notice them is exhausting, too.

I might be dealing with my curse the wrong way. I could embrace my ability and regard it as a gift. Instead of cowering beneath the avalanche of undesirables, I should make eye contact with the entire single male population of Jersey City and eliminate the duds while I have my secret power. Operation Anja Out and About will commence at lunch. It's time I go an earn my lunch, though.

"You do you, Alejandro. I hope your monster moves on and you live to dazzle another day. I've enjoyed our little chat, but an urge to be productive has washed over me. Better I ride the wave before the feeling fades."

"Don't let me stop you."

I dive right into my call list, starting with the printer. My man had shipped the brochures on schedule. The fulfillment center screwed the pooch and let the boxes sit in receiving for an extra day. I suppose Mrs. Cuthbert could blame me for not confirming their arrival yesterday, but what would be the point? Everything's fine.

The last item on her to-do list is to respond to an inquiry someone made on our website. A publicist in LA needs to hunt down a former client of ours. I dash off a note of introduction and contemplate my lunch options. Where do the single men in Jersey City eat lunch?

CHAPTER 16
GRIFFIN

Since I'm on company time, best I don't spend the morning re-reading my text exchange with Mallory, despite my desire to bask in its soul-warming powers. I slide my phone away from me. It collides with the stack of Irma Healy's lost files at the back of my temporary desk. The phone chirps to alert me to a new message, sounding smug because it assumes that I'm unlikely to honor my pledge to ignore the Mallory situation and in desperate need for an intervention.

My right shoulder leans toward the phone while I reach with hands rendered no more useful than a dinosaur's from the way my elbows cling to my torso. Masochistically, I hope she has resumed our conversation. And I dread such an occurrence.

My neutral self wins. The email comes from Apollo Artists, the tango duo's New York management firm.

Well, hello, Mr. Hull,

Thank you for your inquiry regarding the
Canaro y Roca ensemble. My name is Anja,
and I'll be your flight attendant today. Prior to
takeoff, please ensure your tray table is in the
locked position. As for your seatback… Forget
it. Get comfy, lower your tray table, and fix
yourself a snack. It might be a while before I
have any information regarding our former
artists. While you wait, may I offer you a copy
of our in-flight magazine?

Should you have additional questions, you're
free to stay in touch via email or at the phone
number listed in my signature. But please don't
ask me the answer to six down in the magazine's
crossword. It has me stumped but good.

Sincerely,
Anja Lund

My mother would call Ms. Lund a wackadoodle. Her
email rates as the least corporate-toned missive ever sent.
And I'm okay with it, since I'd slap anyone who described
me as the corporate type.

Anja has offered me a healthy alternative to flirting with
my ex, one I embrace hungrily. I shoot her a quick text.

Griffin: Six down: oleo

I hold on to my phone, willing her to respond. When my
phone finally buzzes to announce her text, the alert burrows
beneath my skin and into the bones of my hand.

Anja: Of course! It's always oleo. I'll text you the clue for eighteen across later. Must focus on a different task at the moment.

There must be a takeaway from these disparate, equally captivating message threads. A woman who had broken my heart re-emerges in my life, lightening my mood and engaging me in a way no one has done in years. And a stranger, answering a work-related inquiry, has skipped steps A through X to move a professional relationship from distant to friendly.

Would I have dived in headfirst with Anja had Mallory not awakened a long-dormant side of me? I press the pads of my fingers against my scar. My phone has made my face irrelevant. I appreciate the opportunity to be invisible while being considered a worthy companion. But how long can I hide behind my phone?

CHAPTER 17
ANJA

I want it on record that I have never intentionally trolled for single men on my lunch break before today. If a handsome man happened to be in close proximity to me, so be it. But now I'm walking into unfamiliar territory.

I approach the entrance to a local brewpub and smokehouse. Nowhere near as crowded or as doused in horny desperation as the place can be at night, it still offers a gal an extended menu of manly men. I carve both a path and a temporary silence by watching my feet make their way to a strategic perch on the side of the bar in the center of the room.

"Do you want a beer while you look over the menu?"

I glance at the bartender. Oh, good. We've met before, which, according to my research, means I won't be treated to a voiceover. Phil is flirty in the "please tip me" way rather than the "I don't mind cheating on my wife" way.

"Water. Sparkling with a slice of lime. And I don't need a menu. I'll have the pulled pork sandwich. How's it going, Phil?"

He flings his towel over his right shoulder before aiming the soda gun into a pint glass. "Not bad, not bad. You meeting someone?"

"Not exactly. I'm gathering data on my options."

He places the order for my sandwich and returns to talk to me. "You'll have your pick during lunch. You want me to weed out the guys to avoid? I have the dirt on a few of the regulars."

Oh, Phil. Give me a minute, and I'll have enough dirt to build a community garden. But it could be fun to share my powers with someone without actually revealing my secret.

I plant my elbows on the bar and sink my chin into my palms. "Let's play a game. Point to the biggest jerk but don't tell me why he's a jerk. I want to guess."

Phil grips his towel and scans the room. "I have the perfect suspect for you. He's behind you in a booth in the middle of the back wall. Jacket off, red tie loosened, white shirt."

I spin my seat ninety degrees, raising my head slowly over my shoulder to avoid meeting the victim's eyes until I'm ready. He catches me staring and leers at me with his pint glass aimed at me in a toast.

My pal, the announcer, pounces. "This specimen is mean while sober. His personality does not improve with the addition of alcohol, which he consumes in intemperate quantities."

My hands grip the bar to whisk me forward again. "Yikes. He might be a candidate for AA."

Phil nods approvingly. "Easy call. Let me pick someone with a more subtle flaw."

He walks to the opposite side of the bar. Pretending the napkin holder needs straightening, he takes furtive glances at the personnel before arriving at a suitable target. Mission accomplished, he returns and says, "Second table in from the door, closest to the row of booths by the window. You'll see two guys, both in charcoal gray suits. He's wearing the green tie with blue dots on it."

I shield my eyes, holding my phone in front of my face and peering between my fingers to avoid any intrusions from my narrator. The dude Phil picked has his back turned toward me. I'd have to walk across the restaurant to catch his eye. His companion surveys the room, his eyes settling on me. I lower my phone onto the bar and brace myself.

"This gentleman adheres to a strict three-date rule. Many have tried to break his streak; all have failed."

Too bad, because the way he's crinkling his eyes while he smiles at me would have guaranteed I'd be his next sucker. I cup my palm around the side of my eye, letting it shield me and inform him he ain't getting a piece of this. Through the cracks between my fingers, I spy his buddy checking me out with beady eyes. I remove my hand.

"No woman will ever be as wonderful as dear Mama."

I hold my fist against my mouth to stifle a laugh. Phil laughs along with me, although his eyes are questioning the source of the humor.

I say, "Guy across from him seems too good to be true. Probably a player."

"You're on fire. What about his companion?"

It might be time to whiff. Wouldn't want Phil to think I was a dating savant. "I don't know. He appears normal. Maybe he's a little clingy?"

"He brought a girlfriend here on Valentine's Day and broke up with her before they placed their orders."

"Oof! He must have a major commitment problem and a wussy streak. Bet his mother dotes on him something fierce."

"I wouldn't be surprised. Give me a second. Your sandwich is ready." He leaves me, accepts the plate from a server, and places it on the bar in front of me.

The tempting sandwich persuades me to give my announcer a break. The porky goodness with a side of fries will be much more delicious without an accompaniment of tales of male fails.

"Thanks, Phil. I had fun playing Name that Creep, but don't let me keep you from your customers."

I've sorted through at best ten percent of the men in the room. Didn't I come here specifically to conduct a mass sweep of a multitude of available men? I check my phone. I have twenty minutes left of my lunch break. After wolfing down a too-large bite, I return to my mission, setting the rule to clock each man in the joint, moving on to the next immediately upon hearing his secret. I resume my efforts with the table behind the mean drunk.

Give it to me straight, mysterious voice.

"When he says he's fine with an open relationship, he means on his side only."

"Goes to great lengths to talk girlfriends into making sex tapes. Posts the footage to a secret Facebook shaming group following each breakup."

"He has the sex drive and the maturity of a thirteen-year-old."

I hold my hands against my belly. The men of Jersey City are making me sick, or at least Mr. Announcer's take on them is.

Hold on a second.

Who says he gets the last word?

CHAPTER 18
GRIFFIN

I rifle through Irma Healy's paperwork. She was a stunner, I'll give her that. Someone must have needed to earn a PhD before they qualified to engineer the curls and waves of her platinum-blond hair. And she had perfected the era's sultry squint, coupled with an intriguing open mouth pose for her publicity shots.

I'd consider her to possess star quality. But the competition must have been fierce for someone hoping to be the next Jayne Mansfield or Kim Novak. She and J. Adams ended their professional relationship in 1966 without having found her the fame she sought.

Since the files don't offer any useful clues regarding the rightful owner of the content, I do what any self-respecting itinerant researcher would do; I refer to her Wikipedia page. Irma collected more boyfriends and husbands than roles. The last film in which she had appeared released a year after she left the publicity firm. Her biography grows thin until her death at fifty-eight in her hometown of Kankakee, Illinois. She never had children.

Nothing beats submitting to the Wikipedia vortex, following links from one page to the next until you've lost all sense of time and space. I hover my cursor between the movie titles, former husbands, and Kankakee. Surfing through old Hollywood might promise the higher entertainment value, but I doubt the stars and films would point me toward a new repository for Ms. Healy's materials. I responsibly choose her hometown.

Bingo. It boasts a historical museum. I shoot the curators an email, detailing my trove of materials on one of the most famous residents to hail from Kankakee County (three of Illinois' governors had the same claim). Whether or not they want the stack of photos and newspaper clippings, they're getting them. I consider my Irma Healy sleuthing project complete.

I'm a step closer to escaping LA. The hint of achieving my goal should motivate me to waste the next two stacks while I wait for Anja to share what she has learned about Canaro y Roca. It would mean I could disappear from Mallory's life before she corners me to meet in person. The thing is, I'm not sure if that's what I want.

We haven't yet filled each other in on what we've been doing during the last five years. I'd be lying were I to say I wasn't a bit curious to hear her story. I stab at my phone's keyboard to correct my omission.

> **Griffin:** You might not care, but I thought I'd tell you what I've been doing since we last saw each other. After quitting the publicity business, I've been blissfully unaware of the fake world you guys swear is real. Daphne dragged me kicking and screaming back to LA this week to help close the office. What I'd rather be doing is writing my next book. Oh, yeah. I'm an author now. What's your story? Working on a film?

I set the phone to the side and drag the next stack of files in front of me. Gregory Wilson had fancied himself a silver screen cowboy. Hollywood wasn't buying it. Like Ms. Healy, his career ended in the mid-sixties. I half-heartedly flip through the top few pages, hoping his future will be as easy to determine as Kankakee's favorite daughter's was. The second my phone buzzes, I drop the sheets and grab the phone.

> **Mallory:** I'm done with Tinseltown, too. I'm three years into earning my D.V.M. degree. The best part of my last movie project was costarring with a dog. Even without her puppy dog eyes drawing my attention away from the set, I had already started checking out. Truth is, I love acting, but I hate the business.

> **Griffin:** I feel terrible for being surprised to hear you'd rather be a vet than an actor.

> **Mallory:** Don't. I probably never mentioned my vet dreams to you. It was a lucky break to be cast in *Study Hall* at fifteen. My parents and my agent had spent half my life plotting my every move. It wasn't until a few months after the last time I saw you I had my aha moment, realizing I could call the shots. I applied to a couple of veterinary medicine schools before shooting ended on my movie. And here I is.

> **Griffin:** You might want to check into a grammar class since you're already enrolled in college. It wouldn't hurt for you to sound educated while you explain a surgical procedure to a patient.

Mallory: I find pets are rarely as snobbish about grammar as you.

Griffin: I take it you have never worked with a bull terrier. They are notorious advocates for the Oxford comma. And quite rude when they find one missing.

Mallory: Duly noted. Hey, my next class is about to start. I'm sure Daphne has obtained passes for you to attend every VIP event while you're in town, but if you can give her the slip and would be up for drinks with a grammatically challenged would-be vet, you know where to reach me.

Griffin: I'll check my calendar.

I almost convince myself I will. Why would I forget my position on meeting in public while texting with her? I massage the corner of my left eye, the scar rough under my fingertip.

Mallory: Looking forward to it.

Truthfully, the thought of reuniting with her in person doesn't terrify me. I can't assume a person who left Hollywood behind to become a vet will behave the same way some people in town had following my accident. And she *is* the woman who had once been the center of my universe.

CHAPTER 19
ANJA

According to Mr. Know-It-All, not a single man in the brewpub is worthy of me. I understand why being shadowed by a psychic sidekick could save me from landing in another Colton situation. I've heard an awful lot of deal-breaker material since Monday evening. But will knowing the absolute worst about a man from the start shortchange me from experiencing his better qualities? It will only if I keep walking away. Maybe Violet and Tracey are right in a fashion, discouraging me from regarding every man as a potential husband. Who's to say I couldn't benefit from a palate-cleansing quickie?

I pay my tab, adding on a healthy tip for Phil. In theory, I have three minutes left of my lunch break. In practice, it will take at least six to make it back to the office. Since I'm already on borrowed time, why rush?

I take a detour toward the exit, landing myself next to the table with the momma's boy and the serial three-dater. "You had the pulled pork, too, didn't you?" I ask the man with the killer smile. "I hear Hamilton Pork has the best pulled pork in Jersey City, but this place is closer to my office. Did I make the wrong choice by not trekking across town for lunch today?"

I do not need a stranger to inform me that Hamilton Pork sandwiches beat the brewpub's, hands down, but you can tell a lot about a man who has been given the opportunity to prove his expertise.

Three-dater beams at me, giving me a close-up of his delightful eye-crinkle prowess. He says, "Nothing wrong with the pulled pork served at this fine institution. If you're on the clock, you wouldn't want to rush through the Hamilton Pork experience. Better to save the trip for when you have time to worship. And worship is the right word for their Parish Pig sandwich. Although I sometimes stray over to the brisket mac & cheese sandwich."

I fan myself flirtatiously. "You've made the decision for me. I must give Hamilton Pork a try. What are the rules regarding eating pulled pork twice in a single day?"

Momma's Boy jumps into action, eyeing my waistline to judge me for my healthy appetite. "The restaurant isn't near anything. You'd have to order a car, and then, really, is it worth it?"

The wiser of the two smiles confidently, waiting for his mate to finish his dissent before answering. "Trust me, it is. And I believe the rule is the second pulled pork sandwich of the day must be consumed in the company of someone who recognizes its value."

"Ooh, I might find complying with the rule a bit tricky. Unless… No. I can't be so rude. We don't even know each other."

He offers me his hand. "Easily remedied. I'm Blake, and this is my colleague, Don. We work over at Merrill Lynch."

"Nice to meet you. I'm Anja, and I'm in arts management."

Blake is slow to let go of my hand. "I'd be interested in hearing more about your line of work over dinner. Does seven-thirty tonight sound good?"

"Perfect. Let me grab your number."

I punch his digits into my phone and text him a sandwich emoji to confirm.

"I'm glad I asked for your opinion on sandwiches. And I can't wait to put it to the test. Until then, I hope you enjoy your afternoon."

"The same to you, Anja."

I toss Blake a bonus smile over my shoulder on my way toward the exit. Yeah, Mr. Announcer Man can go suck it. Blake is full-on charming and showing signs he thinks the same of me. I could stand a healthy dose of a man finding me charming right about now. If I go to dinner with Blake without expecting a future with him, I won't be disappointed when the end arrives. Plus, I'll be in hog heaven this evening, sitting across from a gorgeous man who shares my love of BBQ sauce-doused pork.

CHAPTER 20
GRIFFIN

Gregory Wilson, the former client and not-so-slick rhinestone cowboy, died in 1998. The Academy of Motion Picture Arts and Sciences did not include him in its In Memoriam feature. Whether his survivors put up a stink regarding his omission, I could not say.

He must not have resented J. Adams for his role in not propelling his career to great heights, because each year until his death, he included the firm on his Christmas card list. Someone with a sentimental streak thought to save each card in its envelope in his file.

I shuffle the stack of red and cream-colored envelopes. The La Puente address on the most recent card matches the address on his ancient contracts. In a burst of un-Griffin-like enthusiasm, I punch the phone number from his contract into my phone.

On the third ring, a raspy female voice answers. "Hello?"

"My apologies for disturbing you. My name is Griffin Hull, and I'm calling from J. Adams and Daughter Publicity."

"Who?"

"A publicity firm. Am I speaking with Dorothy Wilson?"

"That's me. You're not one of those criminals who's calling to tell me my granddaughter is in jail and I need to wire you her bail money, are you?"

"Not even close. You were married to Gregory Wilson, correct?"

"For forty-two years, most of them good."

"I bet he would have said all of them were good."

"You shouldn't have believed him if he did. No relationship is perfect. Some are better than average. We were lucky. Why did you say you were calling?"

"I work for a publicity firm. They had represented your husband during his acting career. While going through our files, we came across a pile of his press materials. We want to restore them to their rightful owner. May I mail the materials to you?"

"Only if it won't be a bother for you."

"I assure you it won't."

"Then send them when you have a chance. I'll pass them onto my grandson. His wife has done a nice job of preserving mementos from Gregory's career. And mine, too. That's how we met."

"I had no idea you both were actors."

"Oh, yes. I was cast as an extra on a film with Gregory, the first of nearly forty I appeared in. He wasn't the star on my first film, mind you, but him sitting tall on a horse, his jaw squarer than the state of Colorado, and sporting a black hat that would have made John Wayne jealous, well, I fell hard for him."

"I bet you collected an amazing trove of stories throughout your careers."

"Don't you know it. What did you say your name is?"

"Griffin."

"Yes, Griffin. You sound like a nice, young man, and I appreciate you taking the time to call me. I don't want to keep you. I'm sure you have young starlets you want to chase. You don't need to spend the afternoon talking to an old broad like me."

"Mrs. Wilson, I've enjoyed every minute of our conversation. I'll put the photos and press clippings into the mail, and you and your family can reminisce together soon. Have a wonderful afternoon."

"The same to you."

Two down. And speaking with Mrs. Wilson gives me a greater sense of closure than shipping Irma Healy's files to the Kankakee County Museum before receiving confirmation they even want them. Neither project justifies the cost of flying me to LA, though. Daphne worked late last night and has spent most of today out of the office at meetings, so I'm hard pressed to prove my trip is a massive ploy to lure me to her side of the world for a change.

I appreciate Mrs. Wilson's candor regarding marriage. My parents get along well, but to hear them tell it, they haven't had a single fight or wished the other would self-immolate even once. Being an eyewitness to their togetherness still doesn't convince me their marriage is always perfect.

For a while, Mallory and I had a good thing going. I felt understood and supported and believed she did as well. It's no easy feat to achieve depth in a relationship while surrounded by the paparazzi. I grew comfortable with her, and she...

And she got cold feet. I figured there must have been another man encouraging her to leave me, but Daphne's sleuthing didn't uncover evidence she had cheated on me. Mallory wasn't in love with me, plain and simple. She did me a favor by cutting me loose. It just took a second-degree burn and a few years apart to appreciate having avoided growing resentful of each other.

Texting with her this week reminds me of what had worked between us. We don't have a future, but falling into familiar patterns draws me toward her like a moth to a flame.

CHAPTER 21
ANJA

I return to my office, smug for having discovered a loophole in my supernatural contract. I might have an abysmal track record with picking decent men, but I've done fine in choosing men who amuse me in the short term. Should I abandon everything I've learned about men in favor of a voice whose existence defies reason, especially since I'm not going on an actual date?

I haven't done my due diligence in seeking an explanation for why I'm even hearing it. It has to be related to the tattoo. I pat the black plastic bandage wrapped around my calf on my Achilles tendon. Having dropped a sizable chunk of change on my tattoo, even this rule scoffer has taken Amelia and Violet's instructions seriously. Since they say to keep the bandage on for a week, I'm not going to take a chance at ruining the tattoo.

That's what would happen, right? The ink would fade. Or...

Yikes, even my loose relationship with things "normal" people consider to be unshakable truths doesn't mean I believe in magic. Exposing my tattoo to sunlight before next

Monday evening couldn't doom me to a life of hearing mysterious voices. It had better not.

My fingers shake while I call Violet.

"Anja, I have less than a second to talk. What is it?"

"I'll get right to the point. Is my tattoo magic?"

She catches her inhale in her throat, which makes it sound like a hiccup. "You didn't mention a thing yesterday morning. I thought everything was fine."

"Would it surprise you to hear it isn't?"

"I'm at work. This is a conversation for a different location. Tonight at your place?"

"Can't. Date with a hottie I met at lunch today."

"Whatever's going on with you, at least some things never change."

"But you're saying it's totally possible something *did* change during the tattoo?"

"Maybe? I don't know. I need to hear the full story."

"Did anything unusual happen during yours?"

"Not now, Anja. We'll talk later. And don't mess with your bandage, okay?"

"So you've said. Just answer me this: will my life become weirder? Like, will my skin turn purple, or will I sprout gills?"

She snorts. "If you're not already a purple fish, you'll be fine."

Easy for her to say. She keeps leading me in two different directions, implying something might have happened, but then again, maybe not. My suspicion that my tattoo involves magic grows more intense. Whatever's going on, the situation is too odd for words.

It would be nice to discuss it with another friend, but nobody besides Violet would understand my question. I don't love having to figure it out on my own.

Oh, and speaking of figuring stuff out, I should pass on the minuscule amount of info I've pulled on the tango duo to Griffin in LA.

Anja: Greetings from the East Coast. I listened to the album link you sent me. Let me tell you; Canaro y Roca blew my socks off. They landed in the Hudson, and now a duck claims they're his. Whole other problem for me to solve. You couldn't care less, could you?

But on the topic of our Argentinian pals, I am the bearer of bad news: Arminda Canaro died in 1984 in Buenos Aires. I do not believe she has any family in the States. As for Mr. Roca, I cannot find any evidence of his existence, post-duo. The man is a cipher, a ghost. Even in their interviews, he never spoke.

Griffin: Hey, you caught me with my phone in my hand and the urge to find a distraction. Thank you for providing me with one.

Anja: Chasing distractions is a particular skill of mine. I'm happy to offer you pointers. What is it you wish to avoid?

Griffin: Oh, you know.

A bit of text bubbling ensues. I have to wonder whether he took my question literally and is typing the story of his life.

Griffin: Forget my last text. Unless you're psychic, in which case, I'm waiting for your answer.

Anja: Sorry to make you wait. Absolutely, you are right to drag your feet in this situation. In my vast experience, one should never agree to teach a baby to use a pottery wheel. But what's done is

done. Here's how to renege on your promise:
Move. Get the hell outta dodge before he crawls
into the seat. I know a guy, should you need a
set of papers to establish a new identity.

Griffin: Boy, I'm glad we've sorted that out.
Next question: What's your take on
reconnecting with an ex?

My brain wobbles from the familiarity implied by his
question. He might have a suggestion worth pursuing,
though. I'm fresh out of ideas for who else to talk to about
my newfound ability. What's wrong with baring your soul
to a total stranger on the opposite side of the country?

Anja: I'd rather teach a baby to throw a vase. At
my head. I have no doubt a concussion would be
helpful in jogging my memory regarding why
my ex became an ex. You in need of a little
brain damage? Turns out, I know another guy.

Griffin: You know the right people. Which
means I do, too, now that we've connected.
You've given me food for thought on the ex
front. Thank you.

I appreciate your help regarding the duo. I guess
it's back to the salt mines on my end.

Anja: I'm still in it to win it. My company
cleaned house after they moved away from their
Manhattan office, which left our file cabinets
bare of materials from our former artists. But I
love a good mystery. Unless you tell me to
scram, I want to keep digging.

Again, he treats me to a display of dots marching across the screen before he settles on a response. While I rarely have the patience to wait for an answer, I appreciate a man who chooses his words with care.

Griffin: Welcome aboard!

I've enjoyed texting with him as much as I had speaking with my partner in pulled pork. Unlike Blake, though, Griffin has no strikes against him, given the absence of a supernatural introduction. He's restoring my faith in the existence of decent men. Perhaps I shouldn't have blown a figurative raspberry at my helpful buddy, the bodiless voice. Wouldn't hurt to ask for a second opinion.

> **Anja:** In order to level the playing field, what with your baby/pottery tutelage issue and all, let me ask you a question. Let's say you have good reasons not to go to dinner with a man you just met because someone has informed you of his dirty secrets. Would you cancel? I should let you know the dinner involves the world's best bbq joint, conveniently located in my neighborhood.

> **Griffin:** I'm going to have to stop you. The world's best bbq joint is in my neighborhood. Your claims are invalid. But back to your question, which I will annoyingly answer with one of my own. What's the endgame? Will flirting over the second-best plate of smoked and sauced meat leave you satisfied, or do you seek more?

> **Anja:** I'm not sure I should accept advice from a man who has gotten it entirely wrong about my favorite restaurant, but I hear you. My standards for bbq also apply to men. No sorry facsimile of

burger from a fast-food restaurant will do when I crave meat smoked to perfection. Put into human terms, time spent with a man who won't commit to me will only delay my search for true love. Thanks for your input.

Griffin: You're welcome. Now I'm wondering whether my ex has any interest in the providence of her brisket or pulled pork. I believe I have found my litmus test. I'll be in touch in the event I unearth any tango duo news.

Anja: Likewise.

Blake, Blake, Blake. So cute. And so well-informed on the merits of good barbecue. But is he worth my time?

No, he isn't. With fingers rendered floppy from a sense of regret, I cancel my date.

Say what you want, all-knowing voice. I made a mistake by not believing you. Don't let it go to your head, though. If you don't share any flattering remarks about the local men soon, I'm buying myself a pair of earmuffs.

CHAPTER 22
GRIFFIN

What am I doing, asking for romantic advice from a stranger? I conjure an image of Anja, hoping to remove the awkward, mysterious element behind our conversations. She has hipster written all over her. Quirky, confident... Probably lives in Greenpoint or Bushwick. I imagine her to be a tiny woman with a jet-black buzz cut terrorizing the sidewalks of Brooklyn on a penny-farthing bicycle.

Oh, I need to add my idea to my notes. My novel's protagonist will meet his love interest, the woman who lives in a burnt-out building she has decorated with every brightly colored object she has scavenged, when she plows into him on her ridiculously tall bicycle. Perfect setup for an enemies-to-lovers romantic trope.

Which brings me back to Mallory. Are we exploring another romance trope, the second chance? Again, I should look to Anja for inspiration.

Without hesitation, she saw that her would-be date with a man who doesn't commit to relationships didn't reconcile with her desire to form a lifelong union. She spoke my language. I had hoped Mallory and I were headed toward marriage. We weren't.

My accident hasn't changed my romantic outlook, only my prospects. It would be a lot easier to build a lasting relationship with someone I already knew well. Like Mallory. Or, harking back to my conversation with the guy who did my tattoo, I could attempt to build a bond with a woman via texts or phone calls before she ever saw my face. Again, like I've been doing with Mallory.

I exhale, slapping my palms against my thighs with finality. There's my game plan. I won't meet with her while I'm in LA, but I will build on the momentum we've generated in our texts. We can continue the conversation once I'm safe in New Jersey. Months down the road, provided she wants the same things as me—and wants them with me—I can spring my face on her.

Daphne sneaks up behind me and sits on the corner of my desk. "What's with the serious expression?"

"Mapping out my escape plan."

"You can't be leaving yet. You still have files on your desk."

"Half as many as yesterday. Irma and Gregory are on their way home. I have a contact in New York researching the tango duo."

"You'd better get cracking on Celia Hightower, then. Since she's less of a mystery than Irma, Gregory, and the tango duo, you might finish before the weekend. Her granddaughter is an up-and-coming actor."

"In which case, why would you need me to find her?"

Daphne worries a strand of hair between her fingers. "The resolution has an awkward angle."

"You hired me to do your dirty work?" My lips mash together in disgust.

"I hired you to be a diplomat. The granddaughter approached us a few months ago in need of a publicist. K. C. didn't think we'd be the right match for her."

"Since you have an address for her, why didn't you stick a mailing label on the box and be done with it?"

"She didn't take the news we weren't interested in her well. Sending her a parting gift might have read like a slap in the face so soon after our rejection. I want to make the handoff with a human touch, but I have to keep my distance."

"Which means what exactly?"

"Someone should meet with her in person. Not in the office. And not someone on our payroll."

I leap from my chair to gather Celia Hightower's paperwork, which I shove into Daphne's hands. "No. Absolutely not. You're in violation of our agreement. I will not appear in public nor meet with anyone excluding the staff in your office."

"Not even Mallory?"

I hold my breath at the mention of her name. "Why would I make an exception for her?"

"She mentioned the two of you have been texting since you arrived, and to hear her tell it, you appear to have buried the hatchet. It was her idea to make plans. I've penciled her in for drinks on Friday evening at the Surly Goat."

"There aren't enough erasers in Los Angeles County to undo your meddling."

"You're welcome." Daphne winks at me before pivoting on her heels to return to her office.

I can't guess what my sister's intentions are. Perhaps nothing different from what I've imagined. But her methods and mine are nothing alike. One thing is for certain; the goat has gained a companion in surliness.

THURSDAY

CHAPTER 23
ANJA

I plant the bottom edge of Clive Samuels's autobiography on my desk and stare into the face of Apollo Artists' founder. He grins knowingly from the front cover. Mr. Samuels had joined the celestial orchestra years before I began my job.

"Wouldn't it be great to be able to see a picture of an elderly gent hovering above the head of a man you meet in his twenties, so you know what you're buying? I'd love to have a guarantee my future husband will age as well as Mr. Samuels," Alejandro says, leaning forward to enjoy the full view of the impossibly handsome septuagenarian on the book cover.

My shoulders jolt with a shiver. The last thing I need is a second supernatural ability to weed out the field of contenders.

"My goodness, you're shallow. Hold on to the love, and your partner will always be beautiful."

He sticks his finger in his mouth. "Spare me. I assume you took my advice and searched for your missing violinist in the autobiography?"

"What else was I supposed to do last night? I canceled a date with a gorgeous man because he had a serious player vibe to him. Had to drown my sorrows in a takeout order of ribs and a little light reading. I'm debating whether to return the book to the shelf or buy the office a new copy. There might have been a sauce-meets-paper incident on page 173."

"I can't decide whether to praise you for walking away before you grew attached to the wrong man, scold you for not getting something from him before you walked away, or to buy you shares in a moist towelette company."

"The latter. I've washed my hands of casual dating, but I could use help in removing evidence of my affair with a plate of barbecue. It was worth it, though. Here, check this out."

I open the book to one of the pages I had marked, covering a particularly egregious stain with my thumb.

"What am I looking at?"

I point to a picture of León Roca performing with Arminda Canaro before I flip to a photo of a violinist two pages earlier. "Do these two look alike?"

Alejandro pores over the pages. "Kind of? The duo picture is too grainy. Do you have another?"

I type Canaro y Roca into the search bar on my computer. The duo hadn't favored staged headshots, instead relying on photos taken during performances. León Roca had a knack for facing every direction except toward the camera. I enlarge a shot where three-quarters of his face is in view.

"Well?" I ask.

Alejandro holds the book to the screen. "Maybe? But the guy in the book is Lionel Jacobs. He can't be your tango violinist, can he?"

"I don't know. Here's where it gets weird. Mr. Jacobs's career ended the same year that Canaro y Roca formed. I have found zero information about him following his early retirement at the age of twenty-two. He gave his last recital in Philadelphia in May 1952 and then dropped off the face of the earth. No recordings, no mug shots, no obituary."

"Weird. Don't know whether I'd be feeding your conspiracy theory to say so, but both of your violinists are named Lion."

"Lionel, León… How did I miss it? You're a genius."

Alejandro buries his nose in the book. Even though he's not on page 173, I'm sure the smoky goodness of Hamilton Pork's barbecue sauce must be wafting from the current page.

He slams the open book on the desk and points to a paragraph. "Lionel Jacobs might not be his original name. He could have changed it upon signing with Apollo. Clive confesses he renamed several musicians in order for his artists to be more appealing to American audiences. Post-World War II, he worried that in certain pockets of the nation, people would shy away from attending performances featuring artists with overtly Jewish names. I assume Mr. Jacobs might have been a victim of his whitewashing or whatever you'd call it."

"I'm ready to punch the gray fox in his pie hole. You don't have the right to change someone's identity because of your own prejudices and then blame it on potential audiences. Still, this doesn't explain how a Jewish Juilliard grad and an Argentinian violinist could be the same person."

"I'll leave you to your lion mystery. I have three contracts I need to finalize by the end of the day."

"Thanks for your input. I'd better follow your lead by pawning the next round of research onto my friend in LA and tackling my overgrown inbox."

I don't take my advice right away. Instead, I ponder the likelihood that two violinists with similar names and faces could be the same person. Griffin and I have uncovered so little of Mr. Roca's biographical information. It doesn't help that he never spoke during his interviews. He was the silent partner.

Wait a second. What if the reason he never spoke in the interviews was because he couldn't pull off an Argentinian accent?

I rapidly tap three fingers of each hand against the pads of my thumbs. I desperately want to call Griffin with my theory. But it's six-thirty in the morning on the West Coast. Brilliant as my angle might be, interrupting a person's beauty sleep is a sin I don't care to commit.

CHAPTER 24
GRIFFIN

I wouldn't dare say this to my sister, but I couldn't wait to get to the office today. Anja's text—all six words of it—had fired up my imagination the second I read it over my morning coffee.

Is León Roca really León Roca?

Given his tissue-thin bio, reluctance to sit for interviews, and disappearing act in retirement, a name change makes sense. But unless she has a clue to who he was, Anja might have made what had been a challenging task impossible. Texting with her ain't gonna cut it for solving our new mystery.

I dial her number, pressing on my stomach to quiet its nervous rumbling. "Hello, Anja?"

"Hello, California. You're awake!"

"An evil overlord has forced me to keep traditional office hours, and so I must comply."

"I've submitted a claim with Amnesty International regarding similar abuses perpetrated by my boss. I'd be happy to add your name to the report."

"Hold off for the moment. I don't hate being stuck at a desk at nine in the morning, unraveling the riddle you posed in your text."

"Then grab your decoder ring. I'm texting you a picture of a violinist. Went by the name of Lionel Jacobs, but I have reason to believe it was a stage name."

I open my laptop to facilitate the multitasking. The picture on the screen causes my heart to screech to a halt. "This is our guy, right?"

"I can't prove it, but my gut tells me it is. It gets better: Lionel Jacobs began and ended his career at the age of twenty-two in 1952. And poof! He's gone. But he was on the Apollo Artists roster for the duration of his minuscule career. Wouldn't it make sense for his agent to pair him with Arminda Canaro to form a duo if it presented the more viable career path for him?"

With my hand covering my open mouth, I stare at the wall. We've taken a giant leap forward and added to the difficulty level of tracking León Roca. Both concepts enervate me.

I say, "Should we shift our sleuthing efforts toward locating Lionel Jacobs?"

"Sounds like a plan. His bio places him in the US, at Juilliard, to be precise, before his concert career. Here, let me give you the rest of his deets. Born in Queens—that's in New York City for you Left Coasters—in 1930. He attended Juilliard from 1947 to 1951. Oh, and he studied with both Ivan Galamian and Dorothy DeLay at Juilliard. The founder of my company thought his name was too Jewish for people in the Heartland and the South, which means we're looking for someone with a German or Eastern European last name, and perhaps a biblical name for his first."

I don't correct her assumption that I live in California despite my area code saying otherwise. "You've actually narrowed the search considerably. If Juilliard can give me the names of their violin students from 1947 to 1951, I bet we can locate our man."

"Easy peasy!"

I brace myself, prepared to hear the next two words of the phrase, words that make me retch for an inexplicable reason. Anja is silent.

"You don't take the phrase through to its normal end?" I ask.

"Lord, no. Can't tell you why, but I have a zero-tolerance policy regarding the citrus-scented version."

I may have found my person.

Best I don't speak my declaration aloud. "Thanks to you, we're closer to locating León Roca. Since finding him is my mess, let me run with it. I'll keep you in the loop. Meanwhile, going back to yesterday's conversation, did you take your new friend to eat inferior barbecue last night?"

"In fact, I dined alone on a plate of ribs so outstanding, pigs must line up for miles for the honor of donating the next rack."

"It's too early to argue with you over the quality of your restaurant as compared to mine."

"And now I've unearthed the secret to winning any future arguments with you: start early. Not that I anticipate arguing with you, but I make it a point to collect morsels of intelligence to stash away. You never know when they'll come in handy."

"Are you a revenge seeker?"

"Goodness, no. I'm a peaceful, live-and-let-live kind of gal. Well, except for a certain enemy with whom I have a very complicated relationship. No one would believe my side of the story. Let's leave it at him being the person who told me to steer clear of the man I did not go out with last night."

"Perhaps you have an ex who gives good advice?"

"Not an ex, but I can't wait to banish him from my life. Which is neither here nor there. You have an ex, though. Still hoping to remove her from your life?"

"Funny thing is, had you asked me three days ago, I would have said good riddance to her."

"And today?"

"We have potential."

"I'd trade anything to find someone with potential. You have to hold on to it, you hear me? Give her everything you have to give."

I rub my forearm, crinkling the bandage over my tattoo in the process. A tingle courses along my arm, similar to the sensation I experienced at Inklyn.

"Trust me; I won't hold back if she is the one. The problem always seems to be finding someone who wants, uh… well, someone who wants me to be the one for her."

The line goes dead. "Anja, are you still there?"

"Oh, sorry. Everything's fine. I hope your ex recognizes what she's been missing. Spell it out for her; don't pussyfoot around sharing your truth. I'm discovering that, unlike the enigma behind our violinist, mysteries aren't enticing in a romantic partner. Be upfront about who you are and what you have to offer. She'll thank you for it."

My heart has increased its tempo. I press my hand against my chest, hoping to keep it from racing home to New Jersey without me before I take my leap of faith.

"And I thank you for your advice."

"You're welcome. Good luck!" she says before ending the call.

CHAPTER 25
ANJA

Where's a teleportation device when you need one? Get with the program, invisible genie. Rather than tell me the worst about the men of Jersey City, why don't you beam me to LA to meet a man who has *soulmate* written all over him?

Griffin seemed to be reading from a script I had penned. None of the guys I've dated have spoken of The One, let alone practiced the art of not holding back. He has laughed at my jokes, shown creative flare, and been an absolutely delightful conversationalist. Throw in a love for barbecue, and he has presented himself as a far more qualified contender for my heart than Colton or any of the men with whom I've wasted my time.

Is falling for a man I'm not likely to meet part of the curse I'm under? Violet is days late in explaining whatever it is she's hip to about my situation. If I need to create an HR violation at her company to get her attention, so be it.

Better to start small. I text her a lunch invite. She generously offers me a fifteen-minute audience on the bench across the street from her office five minutes from now.

"Alejandro, I'm taking an early lunch. If Mrs. Cuthbert pop her head out of her cave looking for me, tell her our fulfillment house is mailing the newsletter tomorrow morning."

"Is early lunch code for continuing your flirty conversation with your friend in LA?"

I a hank of hair behind my shoulder. "It was a business conversation, should anyone ask. I was simply doing our boss's bidding. Would she want me to cop an attitude on her project? I think not. Good day to you, sir."

I run outside. I have three minutes to make it to Violet's office. Five minutes would be a more comfortable pace, but beggars can't be choosers.

Upon reaching her at the designated meeting spot, I hold on to the bench's back, hunch over, and gasp for breath. "Give me a second. I might have lost my left lung on Washington Street."

"The sacrifices you make for me. I'm flattered." Violet pats the bench next to her. "Let's get down to business."

I take a seat and shield my eyes with my left hand. "Am I imagining things, or did something witchy happen at the tattoo parlor?"

"I need more… Ooh, handsome man alert. Guy across the street at two o'clock is checking you out."

I drop my head further and secure my hand visor to my forehead. "I've retired from hunting for my next date."

"Now you have my attention. Is it tattoo related?"

"Don't laugh or tell me I need a psych exam, but if I made eye contact with the man across the street and he had an interest in dating me, a mysterious male voice would tell me what the man's flaws are."

"Do it."

"What?"

"Make eye contact with him. I'm desperate to know why you wouldn't want to date him."

"I… Okay, fine."

I lift my head to scan the sidewalk in front of Violet's office building. A man waits at the far corner to cross the street. My eyes draw his away from his phone.

"This gentleman puts more trust in his astrologist than in his girlfriends."

I whip my head to the left and shield the side of my face with my hand. "Violet, I'm going to murder you for making me look at him."

Her eyes grow bright, and she covers her mouth. "What's his problem? Are we talking a size issue? Weird fetishes?"

"It's none of your business. Nor is it mine. I hate this damned voice. How do I make it go away?"

Violet's hands drop between her legs. She tilts her head upward and lets her jaw grow slack. "Oh, no, Anja. You wished for that thing you mentioned over lunch on Monday, didn't you?"

"What thing?" I know perfectly well what she's hinting at, but the situation is so weird, I need her to spell it out for me.

"You were going on about drug side effects warnings but for men. Amelia did your tattoo, right?"

"She's amazing. Wait. Is she a witch?"

"I can't say for certain. Did she use a black ink called Magic Mate?"

"Um, I think it was Mystic Mate."

"Right. Here's what probably happened. While she was doing your tattoo, you might have mentioned wanting to have voiceover announcers spill the T on men to save you from the drama of learning their secrets after you fell for them. Only thing is, you could have said you wished it would happen."

"I mean, sure. But I don't believe in wishes."

Or at I least didn't until this week.

"Me neither."

"Then why would you be talking about wishes?"

"I can't delve into the story now. But I have it on good authority that wishes plus the Mystic Mate ink equals a week of living with your wish. Don't worry; the curse or whatever it is will lift exactly a week after Amelia taped the bandage on your ankle. Well, so long as you don't peek at your tattoo during daylight hours."

I bounce my legs, seeking to push my anxiety into the sidewalk. "You're freaking me out. What happens if I don't follow the directions? I have four and a half days to go. You know me. Things sometimes happen."

"I don't know. Sorry." Violet leans over to examine my ankle. "The bandage is secure. Why don't you wear socks for the rest of the week to make sure it doesn't go anywhere?"

I engulf her in a hug. "You're a genius. I think I'll up the security level and go with tights. That'll make them Anja-proof."

"Problem solved."

I scratch my head, inadvertently making eye contact with an elderly homeless man slumped on the bench next to us.

"He was a kind and caring husband and father. With the help of a treatment plan, he hopes he can share his gifts with a new partner."

I shake my fists heavenward. "Great. The first man all week with potential is three times my age and needs to dry out before his first date. No, he's the second man with potential, but I never identified the first. Anyhow, socks or tights solve *a* problem. I'm still stuck receiving constant reminders of how undateable the men I attract are."

"If it saves you from another heartache, it's not the worst thing in the world."

"The curse has sucked away my optimism."

"This too shall pass. Perhaps taking a jaded approach for the next few days would ease the pain. Don't expect anyone to be worthy of your awesomeness. Trigger your voiceover friend at every opportunity, memorize the faces of the losers, and move on."

"I've been waiting for someone who is better than Colton. Days later, I'm wondering whether I should have stuck with the devil I know. Anyway, you have to go be important. Don't let me keep you. Lunch tomorrow?"

"Can't. I have a presentation at one. You had better keep your secret to yourself if you hang out with Tracey. I can't imagine her processing your news well."

"True. We should make plans for Saturday."

"Definitely."

"Thanks for listening to my weird problem. You still owe me, though. I won't rest until you tell me what your wish was."

"We will, I promise."

I raise my finger in the air. "Ooh! It involves Ben, doesn't it?"

"Goodbye, Anja."

"Spoilsport!"

CHAPTER 26
GRIFFIN

"Griffin, you have a call on line three," the receptionist says to me.

I scramble for an empty desk with a phone still connected.

Presumptuous of me, I know, but Daphne's office, partitioned by glass walls to protect her from riffraff like me, is my best option since she's away at a meeting. I sink into a leather executive chair that is far more comfortable than the torture device she has assigned me.

I press the button on the phone. "Hello?"

"Griffin, how are you?" A woman's voice oozes from the receiver on a river of molasses.

"Very well, thank you. Please forgive me for having to ask, but I didn't catch your name."

"Oh, how silly of me. Of course, you didn't because I didn't introduce myself. This is Parker Hightower. You left me a message about my grandmother yesterday?"

"Yes, I did. Thank you for returning my call. We have a small archive of materials spanning her tenure at J. Adams. I was hoping I could meet with you to discuss them."

"I can't tell you how many cherished memories I have of sifting through Granny's photos and newspaper clippings with her. The acting bug bit me early, but hearing her relive her career gave me the motivation to pursue my passion."

"What a meaningful connection the two of you shared."

"Thank you. I must confess, I half meant to ignore your message. Your firm left a bad taste in my mouth."

"I'm sorry you weren't able to develop a relationship with one of our publicists. I imagine you had hoped to follow your grandmother's footsteps rather closely, including on a path through our doors."

"See, you get it. I should have scheduled an interview with you instead of that snooty Daphne whatshername."

I pull the receiver from my ear. "Hull. I'm not a publicist. In fact, I'm not even an employee of the firm. I'm here this week only, helping to clear the office before it closes."

"You poor dear. Did you lose a bet?"

"Worse. I'm family. Daphne's brother, to be exact."

"Now I'm mortified. Please don't breathe a word about my little faux pas."

"Wouldn't dream of it. Your secret is safe with me. Even a lowly research assistant understands discretion is the better part of Hollywood."

"More like the unseen part of Hollywood. Anyway, I'm not crying over your sister's refusal to sign with me. I've found the perfect publicist."

"Glad to hear it."

"What do you do besides search for former clients?"

"I'm a writer."

"Oh, how exciting. Screenplays?"

"Novels."

"I barely know you, yet I can tell you've made the right choice. Hollywood has such a habit of chewing up talent and spitting it out like a bit of gristle. You're above such treatment. Novel writing puts you in control of your world."

"I feel seen. Not everyone understands there's life beyond Hollywood."

"I do. My goal for my career is to carve a space in which to live authentically while I work. I'll only accept projects where I can remain true to myself. I can't allow a role, or worse, a review to define me."

"You have a level-headed approach to the business. It will carry you far. And I'm sure you learned a great deal at your grandmother's side."

"Granny was a wonder. I'm sorry you never met her. I have a hunch you would have been fast friends."

"Speaking of meeting, do you have a moment today or tomorrow for me to hand you your grandmother's files?"

"Today was over before it began. I'm rushing off to a photo shoot and then to meet with a director. If you can stand the sight of me fresh from a yoga class, I could meet you for coffee at eleven tomorrow at that cute place on North Fairfax Avenue, half a block south of Santa Monica. Not the Starbucks, of course."

"Grabbed an iced coffee from not the Starbucks on my way into the office this morning."

"Perfect. I'd love to share my Granny stories with you. There was far more to her than whatever you've read about her in a press release."

"I have no doubt. It will be my pleasure."

"Thank you for ensuring her legacy falls into the right hands."

"I'm glad I could. I'll see you tomorrow, Parker."

"Ciao."

I replace the receiver in its cradle and lean back in the unreasonably comfortable chair. I should be freaking out, having agreed to meet an actor in person. But I'm not.

It's ridiculous for a conversation with Parker to leave me as satisfied as texts with Mallory have. Or my interactions with Anja. To be honest, all my communications with women this week have defied the norm. If I didn't know better, I'd swear a magical spell has turned me from a curmudgeon into an outgoing flirt.

CHAPTER 27
ANJA

S hoot. I forgot to bring my guitar with me today. Not that I'm on the schedule to play for the residents. My volunteer shift this evening is to keep lonely residents company while they eat dinner. I've added a new classical piece to my repertoire since Tuesday. The steady, finger-picked accompaniment of the Romanza by an unknown nineteenth-century Spanish composer, played under a lilting melody, tugs my heart whenever I hear it. I had hoped it would have a similar impact on Mr. Lowenstein.

Forgotten guitars; strange curses. I'm killing it this week. Had I known I was receiving a magical tattoo, I could have made a different wish than for an annoying voiceover buddy to follow me around Jersey City. My new pair of sunglasses isn't doing squat to protect me from making eye contact with a man who apparently embezzles money from his employer or another whose deepest desire is to hire a maid who grants him certain privileges in the bedroom.

With my head lowered to avoid more unwanted introductions, I mull over the Mr. L. situation along the last leg of my commute to the nursing home. I should have wished to clear the fog in his brain and restore his ability to speak. To live trapped in a body without being able to communicate is a torture nobody should have to endure. Way worse than my current ordeal.

I need to help him. The last time I saw him, my announcer friend informed me Mr. Lowenstein had remembered who he was. While recorded music is nowhere near as impactful on healing and memory as live music can be, I could play my favorite guitar recording for him. If my lame attempts at classical-styled guitar playing on Tuesday were enough to rouse him from his trap, wait until he hears Apollo Artists' rising star play Rodrigo's Concierto de Aranjuez.

I breeze into the nursing home, glad to have a game plan in place. "Maria, you're a sight for sore eyes."

"And you look like a Hollywood star. But who needs glasses on a cloudy evening?"

"Shh. I'm incognito tonight. Can't have the KGB identifying me behind my shades."

"And what, the rainbow-striped socks worn with a polka-dotted dress won't give you away?"

I rub my hand against my newly installed tattoo security system. I suppose I could have bought a color-coordinated pair, but these were in the dollar bin. And hello? Rainbow socks with individual toe compartments? How could I not have bought them?

I snap the sock's elasticized top under my knee. "Hide in plain sight, my father always told me."

Maria says, "Which makes me a sitting duck behind my desk."

"You will be handsomely rewarded for your bravery and your service."

"Yeah, right. Let me call my union rep."

"Fight the good fight. I'm going in." I scrunch my nose and struggle to swallow. "I believe they're serving meatloaf tonight."

"I couldn't place the smell, but you might be right. Have fun."

I peek into the room from the door in the middle of the wall. The more active residents have their cliques. While no one sits alone at a table, the less interactive folks could be in different rooms for how isolated they appear. I aim to spend ten minutes each with a half-dozen people this evening. Inevitably, my more social fans will also want a piece of me. Best I visit with Mr. L. first to ensure I accomplish my goal.

He sits across the table from a woman who is feeding her baby doll a forkful of spinach. "Mrs. Berkowicz, I sympathize with you if your child is anything like me. On a good day, my mom could airplane a bite or two of creamed spinach into my gullet, but good days were rare."

She doesn't acknowledge my presence. Neither does Mr. Lowenstein. His chin rests on his sternum. He's outfitted in an emerald-green pullover sweatshirt and gray sweatpants a few sizes too big for him. I won't need to pretend my fork is an airplane to get him to eat his vegetables. He has a feeding tube.

I set my phone on the table and scroll until I find the slow movement of the Rodrigo. "I noticed you enjoyed my guitar concert on Tuesday. Let me share my absolute favorite recording of an unbearably beautiful piece."

After the guitar strums four B minor chords, the English horn enters with a plaintive melody that wrenches every tear from my ducts. The guitarist continues with his simple chords. The harmonies grow a bit crunchy in all the right ways in bar five. I can manage playing the first six measures of the movement, but whenever I try to tackle the embellished melody starting in measure seven, I'm crying for entirely different reasons.

I sigh and sway to the music coming through my phone, but it doesn't reach my companion. No point continuing with this movement, because I'm here for his enrichment, not mine. I switch to the third movement, hoping its perky waltz will perk up Mr. L. No such luck.

Desperate to help him surface again, I cycle through the greatest hits on my phone. A little Beethoven Five, a Strauss waltz, some Sousa. Nothing. Perhaps I was wrong to believe he had found his inspiration in classical music.

He must be around ninety. I play the Andrews Sisters and Sinatra, artists whose performances resonate with the older folks here. His chin continues to press into his chest, and his eyes remain pointed toward his lap.

I pocket my phone. "Thank you, Mrs. Berkowicz and Mr. Lowenstein, for allowing me to sit with you. I wish you a wonderful evening."

Nobody had asked me to perform a miracle, yet I leave their table heavy with defeat.

CHAPTER 28
GRIFFIN

I tap the bottoms and sides of the stack of Celia Hightower's photos and correspondences, corral them into a neat pile, and slide the papers into an oversized Manila envelope. Day three in Daphne's office, and I've rid my desk of seventy-five percent of its dead files. I can devote the rest of my exile in LA to Señor Roca.

Having found nothing but dead ends regarding his life post-Canaro y Roca, I need to try to locate him in his past, specifically in the Juilliard alumni annals. The music school's website is a glossy representation of the superior education they offer and caliber of student they enrich, but its menu doesn't include a listing for locating long-forgotten alum. The alumni page is for alumni interaction; the library and archive page is exactly what its name promises. Where's the Contact Us with Your Esoteric Questions page?

I close my browser. My task would be easier if I knew people who had attended Juilliard. I search Dorothy DeLay on Facebook, not that I expect ghosts to take any interest in social media. And yet, she has a page. I leave a desperate comment, asking for assistance in searching for her former student from the middle of the last century.

With no other viable options, I tidy the tango duo's files on my desk and prepare to leave. "Daph, I'm heading to your house to write. I have an inquiry out regarding Canaro y Roca, but unless it pans out, I've hit my last dead end. Do you need me to take care of the kids?"

"The nanny took Charlotte with her to Liam's swim class. They won't be home until five. Enjoy the peace and quiet!"

"Will do."

I catch a ride share to Daphne's house in San Marino, shooting Mallory a quick text on the way.

> **Griffin:** Daphne mentioned the two of you made plans to meet for drinks tomorrow?

> **Mallory:** I was hoping it would be the three of us.

> **Griffin:** Right. I could see it happening. Maybe. But that's not to say it's an easy decision for me to make.

> **Mallory:** I get it. It's okay if you're still hurt.

> **Griffin:** My situation is more complicated.

> **Mallory:** Will someone be jealous of us getting together?

> **Griffin:** A different kind of complicated.

> **Mallory:** Can't be anything more challenging than performing an adrenalectomy on a bat.

> **Griffin:** Look at you, Ms. Fancy Pants Vet.

Mallory: Still working toward the fancy pants part of my degree.

Griffin: Lifelong dream, blah, blah, blah. What's actually in it for you?

Mallory: Ooh, we're going deep, are we? Fine. Part of what drew me to acting was performing. I thrived on making people laugh or cry and everything in between. And on the set, sure, I'd witness the emotional responses from the cast and crew. But the point of my TV show or movies was to reach millions of people. People I would never meet. I missed having the personal connection.

Griffin: You want I should host screenings of your movies before millions of people and invite you to meet and greet each of them?

Mallory: You'd do that for me, I have no doubt. You always put me first.

Griffin: I'm an all-in kind of dude.

Mallory: I was too young to appreciate you. I let your commitment to me scare me instead. Wait. How did we get here?

Griffin: I believe my driver took a left onto North Highland Avenue and…

Mallory: Smart ass. I was telling you why I became a vet. You trapped me into an analysis of why we didn't work the first time.

The first time?

Mallory: Whoa. I typed faster than I was thinking. Sorry to have confused you. I meant the last time. The only time. Anyhow, vet stuff. I love animals; I suffer when they suffer, and imagining being able to heal them and comfort their people hits the right notes for me. It offers the meaning and connections I had missed with acting.

Griffin: Meaning and connections are the antithesis of the publicity circus. Glad to have left it behind, too.

Mallory: Have you, though?

Griffin: This week is an anomaly. And I've successfully stayed far, far away from the spotlight while in town.

Mallory: You didn't hate attending events with me back in the day.

Griffin: How old are you? Back in the day? Have you chased anyone from your lawn today?

Mallory: Once I find my teeth, I've got some young'uns I need to shake my cane at.

Griffin: Things have changed since the days of yore. Hence the complications.

Mallory: Dentures made a huge difference for me.

Griffin: Glad you're no longer gumming your food. Hey, my driver's pulling up to Daphne's house. Take care. I'll see you tomorrow.

Mallory: You made my day.

Griffin: You should wait until you see me before you declare it made.

Mallory: Connecting to you makes my day. You can't take that away from me.

I wait for her to correct herself. She doesn't. And I'm glad.

FRIDAY

CHAPTER 29
ANJA

With apologies to Miles Davis, I'm kinda blue today. The superpower I wish I had—unlocking Mr. Lowenstein's memories—doesn't exist. Ha! Listen to me. That I even have a superpower has given me a sense of self-importance, as if I should possess a multitude of abilities. My conceit is utterly useless. Like my superpower itself.

Three days in, I still haven't found someone worth dating, thanks to my annoying sidekick's input. I suppose it might exist simply to reinforce the reasons I should reconsider my breakup with Colton. He brings an awful lot to the table. His relationship goals align much closer to mine than my previous boyfriends had. And I can't disregard the way he made my knees—among other pieces parts—quiver. He's kind, stable, and honest, to the best of my knowledge.

I smush my head with my palms. One measly comment about the way he sees me does not a conversation make. Who knows? A five-minute primer on the awesomeness of Anja as she is could persuade him I don't need to change. He doesn't need me to change.

Here I am, privy to the inner secrets of every man who ogles me, but I had never shared vital bits of information about myself or countered Colton's argument. The healthier thing I could have done would have been to have discussed our seemingly opposing points of view with him. How else could I discover whether we're truly incompatible without having responded to his position and he to mine?

My phone buzzes. I glance at the screen, clutching my heart. Have I attained a new superpower? It appears that dwelling on Colton has summoned him to me.

> Hey, I owe you an apology for our little disagreement on Monday. I didn't mean to say you aren't wonderful exactly how you are. Is there any chance I can change your mind about us? The dinner is still on with the client tonight, and I'd love to have you by my side.

His message contains all the right words. I want nothing more than for a man to accept me for who I am.

He might not be the only person who does. Griffin also seems to get me. Boy, I wish I could meet him face to face and hear what my voiceover pal has to say. The ugly truth would rid me of my habit of bestowing upon him a spotless record.

Why am I dwelling on Griffin instead of Colton? *Snap out of it, Lund.* I fillip my temple to restore my focus on the appropriate man.

> I'm sorry, too. Mornings and I are a lethal combination. I can't wait to meet your clients this evening. I'll be at the restaurant early, with bells on. Kidding about the bells, BTW.

I hit send and stuff my phone in my bag. I should have left for work ten minutes ago, but what else is new? Colton has been at his desk, doing important things for the past two hours. Sure, his adherence to schedules and his work habits differ from mine, but imagine what I'd gain by following his wake-up schedule for a few days. Weeks. However long it takes. Mrs. Cuthbert wouldn't know left from right if I made a habit of arriving before nine. Unfortunately, being punctual will have to wait. I set my feet to warp drive to whisk me to my office before my boss realizes I'm missing.

CHAPTER 30
GRIFFIN

Perhaps Mallory has attached a weightier agenda to this evening's cocktail hour. I can't say I object. Have our conversations laid the foundation for me to trust her to accept me?

Anja's advice still rings in my ears, putting the onus of establishing the foundation on me. I didn't present my truth to Mallory. Hinting she should wait to see me before declaring her day made is not a suitable substitute for informing her of how I have changed since she last saw me. By avoiding the topic, I guarantee I will blindside her at first sight. But will telling her in advance create another barrier to overcome? I don't want her to assault me with full-on pity the second we meet. Which brings me back to having to trust she can hack it.

I run my fingers along the edges of my phone to soothe myself while I weigh my options. I miss being alone in my apartment. Days can pass without any in-person contact. Save for quick texts with friends or Daphne, I rarely connect to anyone. I meet my daily word count, check on the status of my sales and ads, and don't for a second miss the outside world. This week has been different.

My phone has connected me to three women. I've lowered my guard enough to encourage the conversations to grow. Each woman has nourished a withered part of me, proving I'm no longer content to play the part of the loner. And each draws me to her.

My analysis should begin and end with Mallory. She alone has occupied an important place in my life in the past. I hadn't meant to fall for a star; I mean, how cliché. But when a gorgeous woman I had known for years from watching her TV series hung on my every word and laughed at my jokes after we met at a VIP event, I couldn't resist her attention.

For the two years we spent together, I had believed we completed each other. That makes one of us. The impact of shocking her with my face will be nowhere near as surprising as it was when she declared we were over.

Plenty has changed over the last five years. What was broken between us—what I hadn't realized was broken— might belong to the past. It's worth taking a leap into the present to explore whether we can improve upon what we already have built.

Before I face Mallory, I have to psych myself up for my eleven o'clock meeting with Parker Hightower. Less is riding on the meeting. I could hire a delivery service to bicycle the files over to the coffee shop and save myself the anxiety of meeting in person. But I enjoyed my conversation with her yesterday, and meeting her gives me the chance to bring my restored confidence on the phone out in public.

I blame Mallory for making me eager to go on my coffee date. Anja, too. They have this way of keeping me on the line by saying what I need to hear. I had no reason to steer my conversation with Parker into personal territory, but upon arriving there, she dispelled my fears. She understood elements of my character immediately. How can I not pin unrealistic expectations of the experience onto my meeting with her?

I receive a message alert from Facebook, which accomplishes what I don't have the discipline to do: focusing my attention on anything besides the women in my life.

> Hi, Griffin. I am the admin for the Dorothy DeLay page and one of her former students. As it happens, my housemate—a.k.a. my mother— was Miss DeLay's secretary from 1950 until 2002. Someone had to tame her teaching schedule! My mother still has each and every planning notebook. If your missing violinist attended Juilliard during her tenure, I promise you my mother will remember him! -Carolyn

> Dear Carolyn, Thank you for answering my query. What an amazing coincidence! Before I scare you away with the specifics that make my question a challenge, I want to let you know I am legit. I am reaching out on behalf of the violinist's publicist and Apollo Artists, his management. I am not a random person seeking personal information. Now, here's my story.

I fill her in on the details, hoping she won't resent me for sending her mother on a random goose chase, searching for a name I do not have. A quick glance at the time, and I realize I need to leave for my meeting. Parker Hightower doesn't strike me as the sort to tolerate playing second fiddle to a research project.

CHAPTER 31
ANJA

I return from lunch, sad to have eaten without Violet and Tracey, my usual Friday lunch dates, but content for having scarfed a plate of piping hot churros. Griffin's text, which updates me on his success in finding a link to Juilliard students from León Roca's class, hits the spot, too.

My pocketbook's zipper pings against the surface of my desk as I fling the bag from my shoulder. "Did I miss anything?" I ask my work husband.

Alejandro's bottom lip draws downward, turning his mouth into a tense rectangle. "Mrs. Cuthbert has been looking for you for the last ten minutes."

"What did I do?"

"Can't say, but I doubt it was anything you should be proud of."

"Drat." I hitch up my knee socks—yes, I bought two pairs of rainbow toe socks yesterday—and put on a brave face.

I knock on the doorframe to my boss's office. "You wanted to see me?"

She pulls her glasses away from the bridge of her nose to peer at me above the rims. "Yes, Anja. Please come in and take a seat."

To look at Mrs. Cuthbert, you'd think she was someone's sweet grandmother. She is a grandmother, and perhaps the gaggle of her offspring's delightful kiddos believes she is the perfect specimen. Her soft halo of gray curls and watery blue eyes, which often appear wide with curiosity above her pink cheeks, mask her inner insensitive drill sergeant.

She passes me an unsealed number ten envelope with our address appearing in both the sender and recipient positions. "The fulfillment center messengered the mailing they sent to our list this morning."

I puff out my chest. "On schedule, as promised."

"The deadline is irrelevant if the contents are an embarrassment to our firm."

"Excuse me?" My heart has gone missing. I'd check for it under the massive desk in front of me, but I am too cold and weak to move.

"You and I proofed the newsletter together over a week ago. Do you remember what we discovered?"

I love writing. And I love writing about musicians. But enduring Mrs. Cuthbert's edits of my writing and her micromanaging tendencies is worse than dealing with my voiceover affliction. Apollo Artists has a very specific voice, and any attempt I make to modernize it is an intolerable affront to her. When she signs off on a project, it's cause for celebration, because putting a flyer or newsletter in our printer's hands means my work on the text is done. In the event she decides we haven't explored every synonym for the word *performance* once they've set the type, she has to live with the results since the only thing she cherishes more than her writing style is saving a penny. The cost of resetting the text isn't worth the price of continuing her march toward fussy perfection.

Which is to say I don't have a clue to what she is referring. "I'm sorry. Could you refresh my memory?"

"Read it."

I pull the goldenrod-colored paper from the envelope and skim through it. Not quickly enough for her tastes, it appears.

"Are you enjoying the section on the Stella Étoile Quartet?" she asks.

I jerk my hands to flip over the page to read the other side. Our previous conversation about the galleys floods into my brain. This is totally our printer's fault. Or was.

I had included the quartet's copy in the version I sent to him. He forgot to include it. And Mrs. Cuthbert's eagle eye caught the omission while we proofed the galleys last Tuesday. It was my job to inform the printer. Except I…

Since proofing the newsletter predates the Canaro y Roca project, I can't blame Griffin for offering me a lovely distraction. Or my tattoo and its curse. No, we've encountered a run-of-the-mill, Anja-kind of mistake. I forgot to call the printer with the correction.

"Anja, I'm tired of having this conversation with you. Do you understand how vital our newsletter is to our young artists? We can't possibly speak directly with every presenter in the country. Where our competitors send their newsletters via email, we stand out for presenting it in physical form. People have a piece of paper in their hand, in a color they can't ignore. The newsletter is perfect for reading in a tiny, unexpected pocket of free time. I couldn't count the number of artists whose careers have taken off because of a spot in a newsletter. And thanks to your negligence, you've robbed the Stella Étoile of their chance."

I stare at my lap, unable to address Mrs. Cuthbert to her face. "I'm sorry."

"No doubt. I've never accused you of lacking the intelligence to do your job. But sorry doesn't solve our problem. What are we going to do?"

"I could pay for a new mailing?" My bank account is on a starvation diet, but this would be the most inopportune moment to discuss her offering me a bump in salary.

"My dear, your plan is unrealistic. You know the cost of printing and mailing a single-sided sheet of paper. Somewhere in that kooky brain of yours is a brilliant solution. I'll be in the office tomorrow morning, meeting with Dame Louise. While she and I discuss plans for her US recital tour next year, you will be at your desk, collecting a list of solutions. You may present them to me after she leaves."

The peasants on staff, including Alejandro, the rest of the booking department, the contract department, our receptionist, and me, have never received an invitation to meet the legendary soprano. I should be honored, but having to come in on a Saturday to fix my mess reads more like wearing a dunce cap and sitting in the corner. Not exactly my fantasy version of meeting a diva.

"Nine o'clock?" I cross my fingers, hoping she'll push it at least an hour later.

"Let's say nine-thirty. Dame Louise will arrive at ten. And now to today's tasks. If I'm not mistaken, I'm awaiting your latest drafts of the Resnick and Mansouri bios plus the copy for Maestra LeFleur's press kit. Please have them on my desk by the end of the day. Thank you."

I bow to her. Awkward, I know, but leaving Mrs. Cuthbert's office after a berating always robs me of my social graces.

CHAPTER 32
GRIFFIN

Points to Parker Hightower for choosing an unpretentious coffee shop in a one-story shack no bigger than my living room. Security bars cover its window, which looks directly into a minivan parked in the closest spot. I take my Americano to a table on the patio wedged between the coffee shop and the dry cleaner next door.

Five minutes later, Parker emerges from an electric car, dressed like a model from a yoga apparel catalogue. Her pale blond hair sprouts from a high ponytail. She has the perfect sort of deceptive face, so wholesome and friendly, you'd swear she was someone you've known your entire life. Her skin glows, but not in a post-workout/midday Californian sun manner. It takes hundreds of dollars and a famous dermatologist to achieve her skin's level of dewiness. It thrills me to link the woman before me to the companionable person with whom I had spoken yesterday.

Partially hidden by a palm tree, I wave the Manila envelope at her.

"Is that you, Griffin?"

"It is."

"I'll join you in a second."

I switch to the seat across from me, placing my back to the street. Parker will come to the table from my right side, meaning my scar will be the last part of me she sees. I have no scientific evidence pointing to this being the best way to present myself, but I cling to my habit, nonetheless.

"I have never needed an iced coffee more than I do today. Six years of practicing yoga did nothing to prepare me for class. Do you practice yoga, Griffin?"

Parker had begun speaking before entering the patio. With no one else around, it makes sense for her to claim the parking lot and patio as her own. I turn to face her.

"On occasion."

"You should—" Her eyes meet mine. She pulls away with a horrified expression and sets her plastic cup on the table to her right. "Just a second." She extracts her phone from her shoulder bag. I hadn't heard a sound, but she studies the screen, pretending it is blowing up with texts. "Oh, no. I have to run. Give me the photos?" She extends her arm while burying her nose in her phone.

I reach across the aisle to hand her the envelope. "Thanks—"

Without raising her eyes toward me, she slides it under her arm, grabs her cup, and scurries to her car. Her hasty exit from the parking lot deserves the full-throttled growl from gunning an internal combustion engine. But like the unexpected end of our meeting, she leaves in silence.

It's been a while since I've endured a full-fledged Hollywood rejection after a vapid starlet had to suffer through an introduction to my injury. Can't say the experience has mellowed over the years.

CHAPTER 33
ANJA

I've made a habit of treating my creativity and pursuit of living without rules as precious commodities that would evaporate were I to detour into the realm of responsibility. What do I have to show for it? An ex-boyfriend who called me out for it, a curse from a tattoo a friend warned me not to get, and a boss who might have given me my last second chance.

The blow from crashing into reality must be more powerful than the restraint of obeying it in the first place. I need to give life on the straight and narrow a try. Or at least a version of it.

The two program biographies I need to hand in by the end of the day don't take long to revise, but I don't send them to Mrs. Cuthbert's inbox right away. She's bound to find corrections, and she'll want the next round of edits returned to her before I leave. No point in being an overachiever. The copy for the press kit for the conductor we signed to our roster earlier in the year is nearly ready, too.

For someone who groans about the length of her to-do list, I can't point to exactly what devours my time. Do I even earn my keep at Apollo Artists, or has my boss altered my assignments to suit my lackadaisical approach?

Colton's insinuations from Monday that I'm not mature certainly didn't sit right with me. My confidence grew tenfold from his earlier text stating he appreciates me the way I am. But it's not to say I couldn't stand to behave the way people expect adults to behave. I'll need to be on my best behavior tonight. It also wouldn't kill me to give it a whirl in the office.

To prove I can be a grown-up, I print the latest updates to Agnes LeFleur's press kit and collate the sheaf of pages with her biography, press quotes, repertoire, discography, links for video excerpts from past performances, and photos. In an act of bravery, I place a printed copy of the mockup I've designed for her page on our website along with the press kit into Miss Cuthbert's inbox. Now, for a reward. I return to my favorite project of the week.

> **Anja:** Any news on our anonymous Juilliard student?

Talk about rewards. Griffin replies immediately.

> **Griffin:** I've made a bit of progress. And now I'm on a break.

> **Anja:** I applaud a well-earned break.

> **Griffin:** I didn't earn my break so much as wrap myself in it and settle in for a bit of a sulk.

> **Anja:** You and me both. I screwed up a project but good. Got called into the principal's office, and now I have to come in for detention tomorrow.

Griffin: You win. The cause of my sulk is the equivalent of a kid calling me names during recess.

Anja: They lied when they said sticks and stones can break your bones, but names will never hurt you. I'm sorry someone hurt you. Was it your ex?

Griffin: No, but the encounter has engaged my defenses. I'd rather lift the drawbridge than meet her this evening.

Anja: Don't blame one person's bad behavior on another. Allow your ex her sense of agency.

Griffin: You're more of a grown-up than me. The business associate who destroyed my self-confidence earlier acted predictably, a behavior I half-expect from the ex.

Anja: What are we talking about? Are you the sort who walks into a room with a whip, cracking it at everyone in hopes someone will fight you?

Griffin: Why yes, I do have a chip on my shoulder. I come by it humbly. My appearances have changed since I last saw the ex. Strangers notice, so I can't help but fear Mallory's reaction.

Anja: Don't give in to the phonies. If a person determines your worth based on whether you match a particular aesthetic, they're a phony.

Griffin: Thanks, Holden.

Anja: Didn't you love reading *Catcher in the Rye* in high school? I couldn't believe my teacher handed us a book with rough language and bad behavior in it. I wondered whether she had read it prior to assigning it. And if so, was it possible a grown-up could actually understand and respect an adolescent's point of view?

Griffin: I'm still questioning the validity of an adult's point of view.

Anja: The struggle is real.

Griffin: My struggle has become less oppressive than it was a few minutes ago. Thanks for dispelling the gloom.

Anja: Happy to oblige.

Griffin: Can I put you on standby in case my ex is a phony?

Anja: I'll also be testing the phony theory tonight. I'll be your safety net if you'll be mine.

Griffin: Deal.

Learning the dirt on the men of Jersey City might prove helpful not for its purported ability to locate my future husband, but in reinforcing why I should give Colton a second chance. If he and I could fall into such easy, soul-warming conversations, I wouldn't need to have them with Griffin. But I'll miss my new friend after we had tracked down León Roca. Perhaps the Juilliard angle won't yield anything, and we'll have to extend the project.

CHAPTER 34
GRIFFIN

I've come closer to revealing the truth about my face to Anja than I have to Mallory. Why? I shouldn't ask. It doesn't take a genius to evaluate the low risk I run with Anja. We'll never meet in person. But I sure appreciate having her friendship this week.

My sister pokes her head out of her office. "Griffin, you have a call on line three."

"Thanks. Who is it?"

"Am I your secretary?"

"You're the best, Daphne. Ignore what everyone else says."

She shakes her head.

I claim a desk with an office phone. "Hello?"

"Griffin, I'm glad I found you. This is Carolyn, your Dorothy DeLay connection?"

"My goodness, yes. I'm glad you didn't report me for being a violinist stalker."

"You're lucky the receptionist admitted to knowing you."

"I'll see that she receives a bonus at Christmas."

"The reason I called is my mother is sitting in her favorite chair with two fingers of Canadian Club on the rocks. If ever you wanted to hear stories from her glory days, now's the perfect time. May I put you on speaker?"

"Go right ahead."

"Mom, are you ready?"

"I need another ice cube."

"I'll grab it for you. In the meantime, let me introduce you to Griffin. And Griffin, meet Edith, my mother. Mom, take the phone."

"How do you do, Edith?"

"Very well, thank you. Lived to partake in another cocktail hour."

"A perfect measurement of a life well lived. I'm grateful you've agreed to help me locate my missing violinist."

"Don't thank me yet. I have hundreds of students in my planners. And I can't read a word I've written."

The plunk of an ice cube hitting the booze and careening off the side of a crystal glass reminds me I'll be facing Mallory over drinks in a few hours. A pre-date numbing session might do me a world of good.

"Mom, hand me your books. Griffin, what years did your student attend Juilliard?"

"1947 to 1951. I suppose your mother's first year was his last."

"Carolyn, do you see the blue book at the bottom of the stack? That's the one you want. Now, Griffin, tell me the name of your violinist."

"Ah, well, here's the tricky part. He built his career under two different stage names: Lionel Jacobs and León Roca. We believe his given name would have identified him as a Jew, and his manager worried it would have impacted his career."

"Oh, what a shame, to have to change his name in order to be more marketable. We've come a long way, haven't we?" Edith says.

I shrug. "It is a shame people judge others for reasons that have no significance whatsoever. But he had a wonderful career. I hope he reclaimed his original name upon retirement."

Carolyn says, "I've found the list of pupils in Miss DeLay's studio his senior year. Should I read you the names of men who might be Jewish?"

"Yes, thank you. I'd appreciate it."

She recites a name. Edith says, "Oh, my goodness, he hasn't crossed my mind in years!"

"Mom, will you be reminiscing about each student?"

"Yes."

"Let's help Griffin, and once we've said goodbye to him, you and I will take a walk down memory lane. Sound good?"

"I might need another finger of whiskey."

"You and me both. Now, where were we?"

Ten names into the list, one triggers my heart to push an extra gallon of blood through my body. "Would you repeat the previous name?" I ask.

Carolyn says it again, and I type it into a note on my phone.

"I think I've found my man. I could be wrong, but something feels right. Thank you for helping me with my project. If my instincts are correct, I'll be in touch once I have more information. Cheers!"

After hanging up, I type the name Carolyn gave me plus *violin* into a search engine. Most of the results are listings where either his first name or last is attached to a person with a tangential relationship to the music industry. My man is a ghost.

By deleting violin, I face pages of men who share my friend's name. I soldier on, ruling out a LinkedIn profile, a website for a DJ, and a dentist practicing in Duluth based on the limited text displayed on their listings. So many men who share a name live such quality lives, I toy with the idea of hosting an event for these gentlemen to meet each other.

But none match the profile I seek. I'm going on a hunch. I have no guarantee my friend ever returned to his given name. Who's to say he didn't invent another for himself after Canaro y Roca disbanded?

At the end of the third page of search results, I challenge myself to keep at it through the seventh page. What will come next, I cannot say.

Amongst the like-named men, I meet several lawyers, a drug-dealing therapist on a popular TV show, a man who signed a hunting petition in Colorado, and a few more lawyers. The obituary notices are not helpful, either. In an act of desperation, I even investigate the Twitter and Facebook accounts held under the same name. When the entries show me men with different first names and daughters who married men with the same first name, I'm ready to quit.

With a sigh, I click an obituary for a woman where the last word of the entry is my target's first name, followed by an ellipsis.

She died three years ago in Jersey City, New Jersey at the age of eighty-six. Listed amongst her survivors is an ex-husband who shares both of his names with my Juilliard violinist. I copy the names of her children. I temper my excitement, reminding myself I have to tackle another round of stalking to confirm this is the man I seek.

I search for the oldest son, Steven Lefkowitz. My pointer clicks wearily on the first five names. None are likely candidates. Number six is a CPA based in West Orange, a town not far from Jersey City. I visit his company's webpage, where a grinning man nearing retirement age greets me from the About Us page. I want him to be my guy.

I send him an email. I bookmark the obituary, close my laptop, and call it a day. Well, not yet. I still have to meet Mallory in person.

CHAPTER 35
ANJA

It's nearly impossible to achieve the look I think Colton expects from me while wearing knee socks. I don't see myself sporting a pair of trousers to a fancy dinner with his client. This is a dress or skirt situation if ever there were one. The risk of exposing my tattoo to sunlight will have passed, but a bandage that is a close relative to a trash bag in appearances spoils the conservative vibe I had hoped to achieve with a pair of stockings. Since I can't find a single pair of tights, knee socks under a long skirt it must be.

Colton has chosen an amazing sushi restaurant in Midtown Manhattan for his client dinner. Commuting into the City exposes me to a host of unappetizing single men. *No, Mr. Voice, I have no interest in meeting a man with a chronic nose-picking habit.* It doesn't matter. I owe it to Colton to focus on our compatibility.

Outside the restaurant, I smooth the hem of my faun-colored skirt over my forest-green socks. He'll have to give me points for choosing these over the rainbow stripey numbers I wore earlier today. And speaking of bonus points, I've arrived before him. I wait an anxious minute on the sidewalk in front of the restaurant. Chances are I've gotten the time, date, or location wrong.

"Anja!"

I lift my head from my phone, confirming I'm in the right place on the right day before I find Colton's text. He swoops me into his arms. I've missed the spicy cedar scent of his aftershave. Not a hair is out of place. I resist the urge to break his brown, wavy hair free from the restraints of its styling product.

"Hi, yourself!"

He kisses my cheek and gives me a once-over, perhaps less troubled by my leg wear than taken in by the fit of my brown cashmere sweater. I straighten my back to present him with the full effect.

He draws his lower lip into a frown. "You look nice. Less colorful than usual, which works. Yeah, it'll do. Let's go in."

I probably skipped this particular lecture in Dating 101, but *it'll do* might be missing that certain je ne sais quoi a lady enjoys hearing from her beau.

He holds the door for me, pressing his hand lightly into the small of my back, and follows me inside. I had forgotten about this habit. While it might offer me a sense of connection to him, it also skews a tad toward possessiveness. I take a giant step, reaching the host stand a second before his hand.

The host leads us to a table where a couple is already seated. I hover behind Colton while he greets his client. His hand pushes into my back, shoving me toward the man.

"Mr. Hayes, allow me to introduce my girlfriend, Anja."

I extend my hand to the client. His hand is squishy though his grip is firm, kind of like being sat on by a beanbag chair instead of the reverse. "Call me Bob. And this is Liz, my wife."

I hustle into the space between their chairs. My hands on her shoulders, we exchange a partial hug. She has a good thirty years on me. I search for a sign of life or warmth in her eyes, but instead, she greets me with a steely gaze. I smooth my hands along my midsection and over my hips. She and I did not attend the same finishing school. Her style is tidy and light blue. Well, except for her brown hair. She might consider throwing in a blue streak to liven up her helmet hair.

"I can't wait to try the food. I hear the chef kills it with the uni presentation," I say, accepting a menu from the server.

Liz shrugs. "I'll stick with the chicken teriyaki. I'm not much of a fan of fish."

"Where are you from?"

"Dallas."

"Do you come to New York often?"

"Oh, no. I don't care for the City. We have everything and everyone we need back home."

"Finding a place imbued with a sense of home is worth it, isn't it?"

"Hmm."

Is Liz the woman on whom Colton wants me to model myself? I would bore him—and me—to death were I to copy her every move and statement.

He turns toward me, lowering his menu onto his plate. "What looks good to you?"

I read the menu. "Ooh, spicy smoked pork belly at a sushi restaurant? I've been on a smoked pork journey for the last few days. I'm this close to continuing it, but their hand rolls are impossible to ignore."

"Let's order both and share."

It's the rare man who offers to share his dinner with me before it arrives. And when he selects both lobster and the uni with wagyu without me having to prompt him, I recognize our bond to be stronger than I had believed. He doesn't want to strip me of my personality; he asked only for me to show him I have the versatility to pivot from fun evening together to dull business dinners. I bear the responsibility of failing to give him the chance to finish his thoughts on Monday.

After our server takes our orders, Bob slaps Colton on the shoulder. "How long have you two lovebirds been together?"

Colton readjusts his jacket. "A month."

"My word, you've barely met. Liz and me, we're thirty-six years into our sentence."

I fight the urge to argue that marriage is not a punishment. But Colton's girlfriend would never dare make an unfriendly remark. "Congratulations. Thirty-six years is quite an accomplishment."

Bob nods, but his eyes don't meet mine. He has ignored his wife since we joined them, too. "You two headed for the altar, or is this just a lark?" he asks Colton.

Colton swallows hard. "I'm at a place in my life where a committed relationship is more alluring than playing the field."

I glance upward, half expecting the words Colton uttered to have come from my invisible friend. They are definitely words I've been waiting to hear him utter.

Liz continues to offer her mentorship in the ways of being a perfect corporate wife. She rotates her body to face her husband, bobbing her head while she listens to him discuss the economy with Colton. I try to imitate her, but thirty seconds in, I develop an allergic reaction to the phrase *earnings per share*.

My eyes wander. We're in the center of the room, preventing me from enjoying a close-up view of the artworks hung on the walls. My eyes catch those of the man at the next table instead.

"This gentleman chooses his dates by matching their physical attributes to the sex workers he keeps on account."

I grip the edge of the table, stifling a groan worthy of a labor and delivery room. I don't have it bad with Colton. At least half a dozen women in the restaurant would have made another man's eyes stray, but the only being beside me who receives his attention is his client. I shouldn't ask more from him. He offers me enough.

I lift my hands from the table so our server can decorate the surface with the mouthwatering bounty he has brought us. Liz gives our dishes a quizzical lift of her brow before tucking into her chicken.

I don't want to be her when I grow up, but I don't expect she is who Colton wants me to be, either. As he generously shuttles portions of our shared dishes onto my plate or squeezes my hand under the table, I realize I am who he needs me to be. I'm glad he gave me a second chance.

CHAPTER 36
GRIFFIN

"Liam wasn't half as stressed as you when I put him on the timeout step a week ago to discuss why it is not okay to rub dirt into his sister's hair. You're not here to meet your executioner. It's just drinks with your ex." Daphne shoves me into the bar, snickering to herself.

I take an exaggerated step to regain my balance. "You're not helping."

A mounted goat's head hangs above the bar, surrounded by a field of chalkboards. With twenty-four taps dispensing an assortment of craft brews, this is a beer-drinker's bar, plain and simple. No purple up lighting on crystal wall sconces, no white leather and chrome. The bar is chill and friendly and not the sort of place to bring a first date. Or try to be romantic with an ex.

Daphne rushes to claim an empty table. "Order a vodka cocktail for me. Anything light and citrusy would hit the spot."

I read the beer descriptions scrawled across the chalkboards. I spot a few favorites. All have high APVs, which isn't the way to go tonight. Nor should I order a pint of a brew I can find at home. I select a saison from San Diego and a strawberry limeade with vodka for my sister. The condensation on the pint glass is slippery under my fingers. I palm the bottom, separating the glass from my skin with a napkin, and pinch the stem of Daphne's glass. My grip nearly fails again when I turn toward our table.

Mallory's hands lightly grip the edge of the table across from Daphne. She has turned toward me, watching my approach. Her face broadcasts her mood. Joyful. Relieved. Radiant.

All her emotions are contagious, but they don't play well with the herd of emotions already cavorting in my gut. With a dip of my chin toward my left shoulder, I present my better side to her. I slip behind the table, still glancing at her askew. "I should have ordered for you. An IPA?"

Her hands smooth the already sleek brown strands of her hair on the sides of her head. She wears her hair in a bun, much better suited for veterinary school than the long, loose waves she favored in her acting days. "Normally, I'd say yes. You know me so well. But I'd love to try the wheat beer."

She reaches across the table, luring me to hug her. I hold up a finger. "Be back in a second." I turn away from her, relieved that I hadn't registered any sign of her noticing my scars.

The line at the bar is short. Before my heart has found its normal rhythm, I have another cold, slick glass of beer in my hand. I set it on the table in front of Mallory.

Without glancing directly at my face, she makes good on her threat to hug me. Neither of us has changed dimensions over the last five years. Her shoulder still fits into the hollow below mine. Her head finds its favorite resting spot against my ear. My hands meet each other behind her back. If something had been off, if holding her had become unfamiliar, maybe then I could have released the breath that has wedged itself inside my lungs. Instead, I suffocate from the perfection of hugging her again.

We pull apart. "It's so good to…" Her eyes drift upwards as she squares her face with mine. She lightens her breath, tempering her motions to avoid disturbing the fragility of the moment. "… to see you."

What she leaves unsaid intensifies my mood. "I had an accident," I say. The words are clipped and too loud even for a bar entering its prime hours. My tone carries a forceful defensiveness. "Right after we broke up."

"I'm sorry. Do you mind me asking what happened?"

Daphne's eyeing me fiercely. She leans forward. "Freak popcorn accident. He was heavy-handed with oil and leaned over the spattering pot. But he's fine now."

Did she preemptively prevent me from sharing my story in full? The way I tell it puts some of the blame on Mallory for breaking my heart. I rub my right forearm. The bandage over my tattoo crinkles under my sleeve.

Mallory tilts her head, gazing at my scar in a way that always makes me assume a spectator is trying to take ownership of experiencing my disfigurement. See? I don't have to look away from it. Aren't I strong?

Daphne says, "It burned his arm, too."

I glare at her. "I'd show you, but my forearm is under construction at the moment."

"A skin graft?" Mallory asks.

"No, a tattoo."

My sister grabs my right wrist. "You've been in LA for four days, and you haven't thought to mention it to me?"

I pull my arm away from her. "I'm under orders to keep a bandage on it for a week. No point in saying anything since I can't show it to you."

Mallory's brow knits. It takes a sci-fi nerd like me to watch the ripples under her skin, imagining them to be burrowing alien beings, and find the whole thing charming. Or at least I used to. She says, "Tattoos heal better uncovered. Mind you, I'm no expert, but provided you don't have an open wound, it will dry better without the bandage."

"I'm following my tattoo artist's expertise. Nothing's festering under here."

She shrugs. "Then keep doing what works for you. Speaking of skin grafts, did you ever explore plastic surgery as an option for your cheek?"

I want to scream, "It's none of your business." Of course, my doctor discussed grafts with me. He wasn't optimistic we'd gain the desired results. Eyelids and lips are especially unwilling to lie still for months on end while the graft heals. Seemed unnecessary to go through the torture of the surgery and a months-long recovery only to appear slightly less damaged.

I stiffen. "I'm keeping with what works for me."

Her palm flies into the air opposite her neck, a half gesture of surrender. "Understood. You're lucky; imagine if you had burned your scalp and your hair never grew back. Anyway, cheers!" She holds her pint glass above the center of the table.

I clink the rim of my glass to hers anemically, my abs contracting to pull me away from her. I suppose I'm grateful she didn't run away from me, terrorized. Pretending it doesn't bother her while implying I could do more to help her tolerate my face is a barely acceptable tactic for a person immediately after they meet me. But for a woman I once loved?

It's not my job to make people comfortable with my appearances. The responsibility of being empathetic lies with them. Yet the burden always seems to fall on me. People resent me because my scar disgusts them. Their suggestions I have plastic surgery are veiled judgments of me for having neglected to care for myself. Perhaps were I to educate people rather than resent them, they'd tone down their instinctive flinching the next time they'd meet a person who doesn't match the standards they hold for presenting a body or face in public. I'm not saying I refuse to be their test subject for practicing empathy. But why must I always be their teacher instead of a valued companion?

SATURDAY

CHAPTER 37
ANJA

I peek at the sleeping Colton next to me. It would be easy to pretend Monday through Friday afternoon didn't exist. Waking up beside him on the weekend restores my sense of everything being right with the world.

I lie on my back, rake my fingers through my hair to spread it across my pillow, and tuck myself under the covers, leaving my neck and head exposed. I cough and shift my eyes to their corners, hoping Colton has heard me. His breathing pattern doesn't register a disruption. I clear my throat with a more forceful cough, which irritates my throat. Now I'm coughing for real. I scoot myself upright to keep from asphyxiating.

Colton shifts. "You okay, babe?"

"Sorry. Did I wake you?"

"Happy to be awake next to you."

"My sentiments exactly. Sadly, I have to go to work this morning. But I don't need to leave until nine."

"I can imagine a few ways we could spend the next forty-five minutes." He rolls on top of me with a grin powerful enough to eradicate the hints of post-sushi morning breath.

My skin prickles, and I scan the room for the reason I'm spooked. It makes no sense to doubt whether we're alone, but I can't shake the feeling. It reminds me of the way the universe skids to a halt the split second before my voiceover dude speaks. I wait, but he remains silent. No, his gig is to tell me the news the first moment I lock eyes with a potential date. It doesn't stop me from wondering how he'd describe the man beside me, though.

I slither under Colton's arm to escape. "To do things properly, I would lose track of time. Soon, I promise."

He flips onto his side of the bed. "And so I shall wait. I am of fan of doing things properly."

"I have noted your thorough and conscientious habits in certain tasks. I mean in bed, by the way. My boss would love for me to bring such attention to detail to my assignments."

I shudder involuntarily again. I suspect my tattoo curse is trying to tell me something. What could be less sexy than to bring Mrs. Cuthbert into Colton's bed? I swear it came from a part of my brain I can't control.

He prods his pillow into a supportive shape and leans against it. "Maybe you should retire your flaky act. The world won't take you seriously if you don't. It sounds like your boss has already lost her patience with you."

The creepy-crawly sensation on my skin settles into my chest. Monday wasn't a fluke. I had the strength to walk away from Colton, but after being battered over the last few days while Mr. Buttinsky blabbed away about qualities in men that sounded way worse than what Colton offers, I've reached a point of defeat.

There must be a happy compromise. The advice I gave Griffin to be forthright with his ex rings in my head. If I don't explain to Colton who I am, I can't learn whether he will accept me. I'd be shortchanging both of us.

I reach for his hand. "You're right about my boss, in a way. Certain projects require the utmost of professional behaviors. And I won't argue with you regarding it being an area ripe for improvement. But doing everything by the book isn't the solution, either. I'm valuable to her because I have a unique perspective. She would have fired me long ago if I wasn't an asset. My life is rich because I put my stamp on it. So, what I'm saying is I'm working on me, and while I appreciate your input, I know who I want to be and would appreciate having the freedom—no, the autonomy to be whom I'm meant to be."

He runs his hand behind my neck. "I hear you. But I know a little more about the world than you. You should listen to me. Last night, you did okay for your first client dinner. Could we polish your image and your conversational skills in the future? Sure. But you didn't embarrass me, and I'm willing to bet you'll be a shining star beside me the next time I bring you to a business event if you'd allow me to guide you on making a few key changes."

I yank the comforter from the bed and hold it against my body, my hands shaking. "I am me. Period. You could be telling me exactly what I need to hear, but you don't get to change me. And because you've told me how you define me, I will always hear your words whenever I'm with you. I'll never be free to be myself in your company. If you can't hang with a person and be cool with them exactly the way they are, and if they can't be cool about themselves when they're with you, then you don't belong together."

I stuff my feet into my used green knee socks, button my skirt, and slam his front door behind me. I had hoped getting back together with Colton would put a stop to the infernal voice from ruining men forever. Somehow, it made everything worse. Despite the confident tone of my words, I'm anything but sure of myself. I'm flaky and kooky. I might want to find a man with whom to grow older and kookier, but men who are interested in the stability of marriage don't want to have anything to do with a mess like me.

CHAPTER 38
GRIFFIN

I should have changed my flight home to a redeye and left this hellhole last night. Daphne had chosen a flight departing at a civilized two-thirty this afternoon, and now I have to pretend last night never happened until she drops me at the airport two hours from now.

I wait until her family leaves the breakfast bar to grab a cup of coffee. She glances up from the basket of laundry she's hovering over on the couch. "Say the word, and I'll extend your ticket. Liam and Charlotte have loved having Uncle Grouch paying them a visit."

"You wouldn't want to oversell it now, would you?"

"We wouldn't recognize you without a bit of attitude. Mallory sure has changed since you last saw her."

"In a way. I'm happy she has found her calling."

"She'll make a great vet." She eyes me, cocking her head. "And maybe a good—"

"Not for me."

I shield myself from my sister with my phone, checking for a message from Steven Lefkowitz, my missing violinist's possible former son-in-law. I had brought the tango duo's

160

photos, press clippings, and correspondences with me when I left the office yesterday. Should my hunch pay off, I can foist the materials onto a human in New Jersey. If not, I'll feed them to my recycling bin.

She tosses a shirt back in the basket, unfolded. "You know what I was going to say?"

"Why don't you tell me why you orchestrated my reunion with Mallory?"

"It was pure coincidence. We ran into each other on Monday, and with you coming to town the next day, it was natural to mention you to her."

"You didn't need to give her my number. Or invite her to drinks."

"What's gotten into you?"

"Nothing. I have to pack."

"Wait a second. Is this about your scar?"

"It's none of your business."

Daphne's eyes spring open. "You never mentioned your accident to Mallory. It surprised me when I realized it last night."

"Why should I have told her? We were over by then."

"If you were so over her, you wouldn't have minded her seeing your face. I clocked you maneuvering your head to hide your left side from her. You wanted her to think you were the same handsome bastard she dumped."

"Are you even listening to yourself? I'm calling a car to take me to the airport."

I leave my full cup of coffee on the breakfast bar and head into the guest room without acknowledging her. Most of my clothes are already shoved into the bottom of my duffel. I dump the rest into it, zip it, and pack my laptop into my carry-on.

Daphne bends her arm above her head and leans it against the doorframe. "I'm sorry if you thought I was attacking you."

"Do I have your permission to translate your sentence to mean you are sorry you attacked me?"

"Never argue with a writer. But you're right. You are you to me, so I don't put myself into the mindset of someone who hasn't met you. Or seen you since the accident."

"I didn't tell you how my meeting with Parker went. You want to hear the story?"

She enters the room and sits on the corner of the bed. "I suppose I can guess. I had put representing my brand front and center. Parker has a reputation for using people and demonstrating a lack of gratitude, which is why I didn't accept her as a client. I wanted to rub it in her face that for even the smallest job, I go the distance to handle details with a personal touch. Ergo, sending you in place of a messenger. Did she say something?"

"Worse. She took one look at me and ran. I'm not kidding; she left skid marks in the parking lot."

"And you're sure it was—"

"Seriously, Daphne. Do you need to ask? She and I had a great conversation on the phone. She was gabbing away at the coffee shop until her eyes fell on my face. Yes, I'm sure. Hollywood stars are all alike. Shallow, cruel people are the reason I fled five years ago."

"I get why breaking up with one star would make you want to leave. But I see no reason for you to blame the entire industry for your heartache."

"Mallory wasn't the reason I moved. I left because of your favorite diva."

Her back buckles, and the bedsprings squeak from the change in her posture. "Allyson Reid?"

I snap the strap of my carry-on and sling it onto my shoulder. "Ding, ding, ding. Tell the lady what she has won."

"This is news to me. She's always so lovely."

"Yeah, lovely, like a rat-infested dumpster. Guess what she said to me."

"Said to you when?"

"At a party you dragged me to a month following the accident. She said, 'Ew.' Didn't have the acting chops to keep a straight face for even three seconds. After using her eyes and lips to express the sense of violation she suffered, she told me Hollywood is no place for freaks."

"She didn't!"

"Whose side are you on?" I press my fingertips against my chest in mock surprise and alter my voice to match. "Allyson couldn't possibly have been repulsed by my face. I must have imagined it. Same with Parker. And Mallory."

"That's not what I said."

"It kind of is. This is my life. Like an uptight English woman declaring an otherwise fine piece of art to be a pity because it expresses the nude form, to many of the people I meet, I, too, am a pity. If it weren't for a pesky patch of skin on my face, I'd be handsome. Mallory was ready to recommend a plastic surgeon to me. Look, I accept my face as it is. What I don't accept is for others to use it as the primary means of judging me."

I grab my duffel, desperate to leave Daphne—and LA— behind.

CHAPTER 39
ANJA

The single men of Jersey City have no right to be awake before noon on a Saturday. Shouldn't the guy who, according to my curse, "won't lift a finger to help anyone besides himself" still be unconscious at this hour? I give each undesirable man I pass my "gargling curdled milk" face as I walk from Colton's apartment to the Apollo Artists office.

Residual quivers and trembles from my conversation with Colton continue to plague my extremities and my gut. I shouldn't have settled for him. But what other options do I have? My warning label reader has proven the majority of men are undateable, and most likely, so am I. The sole change I've experienced from my curse is feeling a whole lot worse about myself than I did after walking out on Colton on Monday.

That said, storming away from my ex today has its benefits. A more passionate goodbye might have disrupted my schedule, giving my boss more ammunition to use against me. Thanks to my speedy exit, I spend five minutes in the hallway, waiting for Mrs. Cuthbert to arrive with the keys to the office.

"Well, this is a surprise. Aren't you the early bird?" she trills as she exits the elevator.

"I know your time is valuable."

"Not only mine, dear. Time itself is valuable. Now tell me about the Agnes LeFleur press kit you sent me. Is the single page with her photos and the quotes live on our website?"

Great. By making the extra effort to show her how the press kit will appear on our site, I set myself up for an unnecessary round of critiques. "No. I formatted the information to resemble a webpage, but I'll leave uploading the final version to our webmaster."

"Does the abundant amount of white space cost us money?"

Mrs. Cuthbert takes a maximalist approach to designing our flyers and brochures. She crams all the info she can onto the smallest sheet of paper. Getting her money's worth is her favorite hobby.

"Web design differs from print design. We pay for hosting and… I don't want to bore you with the digital end of things. The biggest chunk of our budget goes to our web designer. He bills us by the hour, which means we can cut costs by giving him exactly what we want him to post and making fewer changes. A page with a clean design and less content might cost less than a page dense with information because it takes less time to program."

"What you sent me was incredibly elegant, almost soothing. I lingered on the page. I trust the actual version will have places people can click to receive more information?"

"Exactly. Each link will lead a visitor to the elements of her press kit, which they can then download. And thank you for your kind words."

"I'm not a fan of computers or phones that know more than me, but this old dog might have learned a new trick.

We should design more of our materials to have the same modern, elegant aesthetic. Can you design your correction for our newsletter to resemble a webpage?"

"Absolutely. It's a wonderful idea."

I'm not just blowing smoke up my boss's skirt to keep the good juju flowing. She has made my job much easier by allowing me to design it according to my style. I can whip together my version of the newsletter omission in my sleep.

"Then you get to work. No, first please put the kettle on. Dame Louise will want a mug of chamomile tea immediately upon her arrival. It must steep for five minutes. Do not overheat the water. She only takes honey in her tea, but you must present her with cream and two slices of lemon anyway. While she is quite particular, she dislikes being aware of the efforts people make to cater exactly to her desires." If I'm not mistaken, my boss rolled her eyes at the end of her instructions.

Trust me, Mrs. Cuthbert. I know from people who demand perfection.

I play the role of simpering servant when the legendary soprano makes her entrance. After presenting her with tea service even the Queen of England couldn't fault, I back out of the room, this close to bowing to her with each step.

I shuffle to my desk, missing the buzz of my coworkers. I've never come to the office on the weekend. Why would I?

One thing is certain: I need to kill it on the Stella Étoile Quartet newsletter. Colton is wrong about me. I can produce professional-level results on my own terms.

I dig through my email folder to find the copy that should have appeared in our printed newsletter. It comprises a paragraph of text and a thumbnail photo. I paste both onto a blank page and craft an intro paragraph with a touch of the apology I'm sure Mrs. Cuthbert believes I owe the subscribers to our mailing list. I assume she'll approve what I've created. Why not drop the copy I've printed in her inbox and leave?

Colton has me fired up to prove I'm better than the way he defines me. Who is he to say I'm not "professional"? Okay, my boss has made similar comments. And I deserve her criticism whenever I torpedo a project. But we get to where we need to be in the end. Sometimes we even land in a better place than she had imagined. Details matter to me, but I tend to notice the details other people have missed. Or don't pay attention to the details that aren't as important as people want them to be.

I sign into our company's email marketing account, the least utilized tool at Apollo Artists. We haven't yet even designed a template with our logo. Our administrative assistant updates the mailing list regularly, but if we send even half a dozen mailings a year, I'd be surprised.

It takes twenty minutes for me to create a modern template with our logo, the copy from the newsletter, two additional photos, a link to the quartet's repertoire, and a call to action at the end. Rereading the stilted, formal text, I take a leap of faith.

The string quartet keeps an active profile on Instagram. Their curated content is professional, but the voice behind their posts is Millennial, not early Baby Boomer. For instance, rather than announce that their debut recording is forthcoming, as the newsletter copy declares, they share fifteen-second clips, refer to the tracks being in the can, and use the hashtag "exhausted."

I scrape several recent posts, choosing content related to the points we're highlighting in our newsletter to reshape the copy into a better representation of who our artists are. I expect Mrs. Cuthbert to scowl at me over the top of her glasses, but I have an opening to offer my vision. No way I'm letting it slip away.

I add the second version to my boss's inbox, swiveling my head toward her office. I can't accomplish anything more with my masterpiece until her meeting ends.

In my effort to prove I'm not a total basket case, I had emptied my inbox yesterday afternoon following my dressing down. The only outstanding project I have is to help Griffin find our tango violinist. He has been mum on the subject since yesterday. Probably got lucky with the ex and has forgotten about me. I have no rational reason for it, but my stomach turns into a jealous jumble of knots when I consider him having someone else he'd rather talk to.

CHAPTER 40
GRIFFIN

Nothing like killing an extra hour at LAX with new reading material in the form of texts from a pair of women who suspect they owe you an apology but haven't yet figured out why. I read the texts with a sigh.

> **Daphne:** I'm sorry you left before I could get to the bottom of exactly why you're upset with me. Please call me.

> **Mallory:** Thanks for coming last night. Is it me, or had we been doing better in the catching-up department before shifting from our phones to RL? Let's keep in touch.

My diatribe in Daphne's spare room echoes in my mind like a fever dream. I hadn't realized how much Parker and Mallory had hurt me. My sister doesn't deserve to be on the receiving end of the rage I had intended for them, but she played a role in prompting me to unleash it.

She showed her hand. I suspect she had dreamed of a reconciliation between Mallory and me and did everything in her power to bring it to fruition, including luring me to LA. And stupid me, I had hoped for the same. I suppose I'm angry with myself, too.

My irrational wish to connect to Mallory before we met in person lines up with what I had said to Curly at the tattoo studio on Monday. I made a misguided wish to bypass the Allysons, the Parkers, and the Mallorys by forging an incredible bond, sight unseen, with a woman who would not judge me by my scars. Had Mallory and I spent months cultivating our relationship online, would our first post-breakup face-to-face meeting have gone differently?

My phone buzzes at me, and I give it a disgruntled glance, expecting another pestering text from my sister. It's from Anja.

> **Anja:** Since I didn't see the bat signal last night, I assume everything was hunky dory with the ex?

> **Griffin:** Quite the opposite. Licking my wounds as we type.

> **Anja:** Bummer. Should I send a condolence gift? Balloons, perhaps?

> **Griffin:** Give me a hundred of those suckers and a pin, and maybe my mood will lighten once I'm standing in a puddle of balloon shards. How did things go for you?

> **Anja:** My ex has retained his ex status following a spectacular display of why he doesn't deserve me.

Griffin: Sorry, but perhaps not. You don't sound devastated. Is your self-confidence available in a lending library? I could stand a dose.

Anja: I've borrowed it from the most unexpected source: my boss. I offered her a solution to a disaster of my making, and now she thinks I'm a genius. Can I solve any problems for you while I'm still on my ego trip?

Griffin: Glad you asked. How important are a man's looks?

Anja: Do you mean, have I dated men whose faces and bodies tempted me to come closer in the first place? Yes. But in the grand scheme of things, the fact that I'm single proves the unimportance of physical attributes. Attraction is easy; a cute elbow here, a button nose there, throw in a spray of pheromones. Poof! Experiencing physical attraction isn't a wondrous accomplishment. You know what's unattractive? Men who fail to see me underneath my packaging.

I swallow hard before rereading her last text.

Griffin: I can't believe you wrote that.

Anja: Am I wrong?

Griffin: No. You're brilliant.

Anja: Careful. My head is already unmanageably large at the moment.

Griffin: Let's change brilliant to psychic. I just lost my cool for the same reason. Not for being psychic. For being misjudged. I wonder if you should send balloons to my sister to apologize for my behavior. Or teach me your Zen-like ways.

Anja: I believe you still need the balloons. You can invite her to help you pop them. You'll both feel better.

Griffin: As you may have deduced, my ex and yours have a lot in common. How do you recover from having someone judge you for the wrong reasons?

Anja: Wow. I wouldn't say I'm ever over it. Because I'm accustomed to being the person who disappoints, I usually back away and move on. I bought two pairs of silly socks on Thursday. They make me happy. And I'm having dinner with my two BFFs tonight. No harm can come to me when I'm with them.

Griffin: I want to revisit what you said about you being a disappointment to people. Your comment makes me sad.

Anja: Don't let it. I'm your basic heptagonal peg living in a world of square holes. I rarely follow the tried-and-true path. And sometimes, I don't wind up where I should. I'll always take responsibility for making a mess of things, though. The people who love me don't try to change me. Everyone else keeps me around for their amusement until I'm an inconvenience. I've decided I don't need such people in my life.

Griffin: Good riddance to them! I wish I could eliminate them before I let them get close to me.

Anja: Ooh, careful what you wish for. I can't explain my current situation to you but trust me; upon sweeping away the garbage people before they stink up your life, you might find yourself painfully alone. I suspect a little of their stench would go a long way toward reminding you why you're a kick-ass human being.

Griffin: Do you give TED Talks?

Anja: I'd probably forget to hit record.

Griffin: I've put you on the spot with my tough questions. You're more than welcome to level the playing field. Hit me with a question or two.

Anja: Hmm. Are you the type who shudders when asked what he'd do on his last day alive?

Griffin: No. It's an easy question. I'd surround myself with a sampler plate from my favorite barbecue restaurant, a bottle of an aged single malt, a couple of Jules Verne novels, maybe take the occasional glimpse at a mind-blowing photo of Earth from outer space to remind myself how insignificant one human being on a small planet truly is, and, well, sayonara.

Anja: Commendable. We've never discussed Jules Verne. I damned near exploded the first time I read *Around the World in 80 Days*. I'm still waiting for someone to whisk me away on such an adventure. And I love imagining how new and thrilling the scientific discoveries he detailed in each of his books must have been during his era. Good stuff!

Griffin: I haven't told you I write fiction, have I? Steampunk, to be exact.

I stare at my phone, waiting for her response, but the conversation has gone quiet. Since they've begun boarding my flight, the timing of her disappearance suits my schedule. Before I shove my phone into my jacket pocket, it buzzes again.

Anja: Sorry to leave you hanging for a couple of minutes. I was busy loading three of your novels onto my e-reader. Why have you held out on mentioning your books? I'm your target demographic.

Griffin: I guess it never seemed relevant. Since you are a fan of steampunk, what's your take on penny farthing bikes? Would you ride one? Have you ever wished you could build a home in a burnt-out building and decorate it with colorful fabrics and bits of metal you hope to turn into a whimsical vehicle?

Anja: It's like you know me.

Griffin: I'm learning that it takes more than a meaningful text exchange to know a person.

Sorry. My bitterness has nothing to do with you. Never mind. I have to run. I'll be in touch with the next round of progress on my León Roca lead.

Anja: Don't let me keep you.

Man, if I didn't know better, I'd swear magical forces were at work, putting each woman I communicate with through an irresistible filter meant to lure me into hoping she might be the woman of my dreams. I close the message app and open my boarding pass. No matter how perfect Anja appears to be, I'm not falling for this bond-by-text scheme again.

CHAPTER 41
ANJA

"Tracey, you're the color of whatever the green stuff we're eating is. What's wrong?" I ask.

Tracey, Violet, Ben, and I sit around a low table decorated with mounds of Ethiopian food spread on a table-sized layer of injera.

Tracey juts her chin toward the space between Violet and my shoulders. "Voldemort."

In the least slick move possible, Violet and I whip our heads behind us. Nick, the man Tracey almost married, has his paws clamped around the elbow of a busty brunette he's guiding to a table not far from ours. He's too enraptured by her body to notice us gawking. Violet and I close ranks to protect our bestie from his sight.

Tracey ducks. "I seem to have lost my appetite."

I reach across the table for her hand. "Should we ask our server to move us to another table? Heck, the beauty of eating without plates and silverware is a pair of people can pick up the table itself and haul it to a quiet corner far from the gateway to hell."

"I don't want to make a fuss. Let me slink away before the devil spots me. Sorry to ruin dinner."

"Nothing's ruined. The mush can take it. Do you want us to bring you a doggy bag?" I ask.

"Nah. I'll send you money for my share of the bill."

Ben reaches for her elbow. "Dinner's on me."

"Man, you are the best! Violet, I'm glad you didn't listen to me the first time I met him. See you soon." She swings her chair one hundred-eighty-degrees and slinks away from the table with her spine contorted into a dramatic S-shape to lower her profile.

Violet, Ben, and I create a shield to prevent the ex from noticing her. Once she has safely departed, I say, "Ugh. Let's hope he doesn't recognize us. I don't want to speak to the jerk. But I suppose it would have been worse if Tracey had to say hi to him. I wouldn't want to be her in that situation."

Violet and Ben's heads snap toward each other, their eyes wide. She says, "Yeah, you don't want to be anyone besides yourself. Trust me."

Ben elbows her. "Come on. It wouldn't be the worst thing to be someone else for a week, would it?" I catch a wink he intended only for her.

I lean forward. "I have a sneaking suspicion you two have discussed body swaps before."

Violet lowers her forehead into her palm. She swivels her head toward Ben, scrunching her nose. "You remember that hearing voices thing Anja told me?"

I jump into their private conversation. "Wait, you shared my completely bizarre, unprovable experience with him?"

Ben nods, keeping his eyes on Violet while his chin points at me. "You can tell her."

"Tell me what?" I take a giant gulp of water.

Violet's shoulders rise with her breath. "We have every reason to believe there's something fishy about the Mystic Mate tattoo ink."

"Fishy how? Amelia told me it was vegan."

"Ben and I both phrased a thought as a wish while we were being tattooed with the ink. The same thought. We both said…" She rubs the tattooed violets on her left arm and lowers her voice. "We wished we could see ourselves differently. I meant it to understand why my boss didn't value me. Of course, that turned out to be entirely on him. Ben wanted to see the progress of the tattoo on his calf. Anyway, um, you don't have to believe it. We won't take offense."

"No! Did you two swap bodies?" My mouth hangs open. "Holy moly! You did! It all makes sense now. When Violet did shots with the strange men at the rooftop bar, that was you, Ben?" He nods. "Who were Tracey and I talking to during our intervention?"

Ben thumps his chest. "Still me. We swapped back twenty-four hours later."

"I have many, many follow-up questions about your experience, but I want to focus our conversation on my current problem. What you're saying is I'm under a spell because I wished men came with warning labels?"

"That's about the size of it," Violet says.

"Make it go away!"

"Can't. You must gut it out until exactly a week after Amelia bandaged you."

"I'm supposed to remember when that was? Okay, let me try. I know I had a five-thirty appointment on Monday. I think she said the tattoo would take up to two hours? Thanks to my brush with magic, I was a tad dizzy. Time meant nothing to me."

"You don't require a magic spell to achieve such a state." Giggling into her fist, Violet is altogether too pleased with her jab.

"Yeah, thanks, friend."

"You know I love you! As for when to un-bandage, better to err on the side of caution. Remove your bandage at eight on Monday. Our lucky time." She and Ben dive toward each other for a kiss.

"I'm guessing you have a watch store's worth of times you've gotten lucky ever since. Jealous. No, not because I want to do either of you. It has been a sucky week with men, and my curse buddy makes the whole 'finding the one' ordeal seem futile."

"There's always the homeless dude from Thursday. You also mentioned a guy at the tattoo gallery who came with a decent recommendation. Two potential mates in a week is a viable ratio."

I shove a piece of injera topped with medium-brown mush into my mouth. Boy, they've packed amazing flavors into our dishes, even if I have no idea what I'm actually eating. Warm, bright... Which sounds like...

Yo, announcer dude. I've given you the start of a description for a desirable man. Finish it and fetch him for me, would you?

"And yet I haven't talked to either of them. The only man worth meeting isn't an option."

"Why not?" Ben asks.

"For starters, he's in LA. Well, distance is the only reason I have, but three thousand miles separating us is reason enough."

That and the abrupt way he ended our last text session.

SUNDAY

CHAPTER 42
GRIFFIN

Alone in my apartment in Jersey City after a fitful sleep, I'm ready to put the last week behind me. My text exchange with Anja had haunted me the entire flight home, disrupting my plans to write. Even plugging her energy into the character I've developed as a love interest for Talib didn't feel productive. I sensed I was creating her for me, not for him.

And that's not how I want to play it, like Pygmalion, sculpting the love of my life. I had tried this approach with Mallory over the last few days, but no amount of flirting with her via text messages could erase our history or alter the way she sees me in the present. I don't have the power to chisel away the parts of her I don't like.

Embarrassingly, my Pygmalion complex extends beyond Mallory. I am guilty of willing Anja to stand in for her. In reestablishing a bond with my ex, I had engaged my limbic system, processing every exchange I had with any woman through a romantic filter. So what if Anja says the right things and does them in an engaging style? I've imagined her to have a purpose in my life far different from the reason we have been in touch. The second I decided to use her personal phone number on Tuesday instead of her corporate email address, I reassigned her from the role of business contact to potential girlfriend.

I had better find León Roca—fast—before I let Anja sweep me away.

At least I might have made a bit of progress on the tango front. Steven Lefkovitz had left me a voicemail while I flew home yesterday, telling me his ex-father-in-law is still alive. He has offered to help me determine whether I have found my man.

I sip my mug of coffee in my quiet apartment, staring down an empty schedule. The day is bright, but I leave my curtains closed rather than allow sunlight to lift the gray shadows from my drab living room.

I could afford to replace the secondhand couch I bought five years ago. One of these days. The couch, leather-adjacent and the color of congealed fat clinging to the sides of a plastic container of chili, is a poor match for the wingback chair upholstered in grayish cream (formerly white?), burgundy, and hunter-green stripes. The overflowing bookcase and a sculpture built from gears, bicycle chains, and ball bearings would tell a visitor what I want them to know about me, but guests would be correct in assuming the ugly, beat-up furniture completes my story.

Like my scar.

I slap my hand on the kitchen counter, putting my pity party behind me. Best way to wrestle my brain into working order is to move forward. I grab my phone to listen again to Steven Lefkovitz's message before hitting the call button.

He answers, "Hello?"

"Hi, this is Griffin Hull. Thanks for returning my call."

"Your message intrigued me, reminding me how little I knew my father-in-law while he and my mother were married. They met at a nursing home three years before she died. My sisters never supported their courtship and subsequent marriage, but Mom was sharp. I trusted her decision and appreciated the spark Jacob brought into her life."

"Companionship is everything, especially in old age."

"Exactly. My sisters didn't agree. They thought my mother's new spouse would bleed her dry. There wasn't much money to fight over, and I assumed Mom would use most of her assets to provide care for herself. Nor did we have any information regarding the health of his estate. Anyway, their marriage was brief, less than two years. One of my sisters had power of attorney and used it to file a divorce on my mother's behalf. My mother died six months later. I don't know whether she was aware of the divorce; regardless, she and Jacob continued to share a room. He must have been in the early stages of dementia when they met, and he continued to drift further and further away. I've visited him once since the funeral, but he didn't know me."

"Was he a musician?"

"Honestly, the little I knew of him was based on who he was in the present. My mother spoke about how listening to music always perked him up, but she never mentioned his career. You said you're searching for a violinist?"

"Yes. Does your father-in-law have any living relatives?"

"To the best of my knowledge, no. My mother delighted in telling me she was his first wife. I can imagine a busy touring career would interfere with building a family."

"None of the biographical materials I have for my violinist mentions a family, either. I don't want to raise my hopes, but nothing I've learned about your father-in-law disputes my theory that he could be the missing member of my tango duo. May I visit him?"

"I don't see why not. I'll call the home to let them know I've sent you. That said, it has been over a year since I last visited him, and he was not in great shape then. I wish I could give you the secret to reaching him, but I'm at a loss. Even if you don't find the answers to your questions, I bet you'll bring comfort to a lonely old man."

"Not a bad prospect. I appreciate everything you have done for me. I'm glad your mother found someone to share her last years with. Take care."

I hang up, unsure whether a visit to the nursing home will bring closure to my Canaro y Roca project. Regardless, I'll gladly welcome embarking on the next leg of my wild goose chase to locate my tango violinist. Anything that can distract me from reading through the miles of texts from Anja I have accumulated over the last few days will do me a world of good.

CHAPTER 43
ANJA

In the Anja-through-the-looking-glass world into which I've fallen, I'm in danger of being early yet again. Who'd believe I could teach the White Rabbit a trick or two about punctuality? The folks at the nursing home don't want this addled version of me arriving early, that's for sure. I don't need to leave home until two-fifteen for my three o'clock song fest, yet I'm ready and feeling stir-crazy.

The sky has out-blued itself today, stretching in a crisp, clear blanket above Jersey City in contrast to the thick, gray fog enshrouding me. My mood could stand a little sunshine. I grab my guitar and head to Hamilton Park to banish a woe or two before heading to the home.

Kids holler and whiz around the playground. Not my speed today. I plop myself on the steps leading to the gazebo in the center of the park. They're cold on the tush, but I already feel better being outside the constricting walls of my apartment.

A few weeks ago, Tracey, Violet, and I had made a pledge to change our lives. Violet, wallowing in the misery of working for the world's worst boss, vowed she would quit her job. A week later, her boss committed a fireable offense, she landed a sweet promotion into her dream job, and oh, bonus, now has the most amazing, studly boyfriend. As it turned out, none of these transformations had anything on the secret she and Ben had been keeping from me.

Anyway, I'm dwelling on our pledge because Tracey had promised she'd dip her toe into the dating pool now that her heart has healed after Nick trashed it a year ago. I hope her near miss with him last night hasn't torpedoed her plans. And I, a disaster on wheels when it comes to picking men, even with my supernatural power, haven't made good on my pledge, either.

A streak of blue and gray draws my eyes from the folds of my purple and gold skirt and my mind away from unkept promises. My gaze connects with a middle-aged man passing by.

"This gentleman's ex-wife filed for a restraining order after seeking a divorce. She wasn't the first to do so."

I slam my palm against my eyelids, holding my breath and counting to ten before I open my eyes again. The man has continued walking. I add his warning label to the ever-growing list I've been keeping in a small notebook.

I flip to the first page to read where it all began. The statements I heard at the tattoo gallery are approximations of what I remember; except for one, they barely differ from the rest of the descriptions in my book.

"Married but not monogamous."

"Breast man who doesn't learn his girlfriends' names."

"Honest, funny, and values inner beauty."

"Kinky in a selfish way."

I don't deserve a man who will cheat on me or who will see me only as a collection of body parts. I'm not irrational to want an honest, devoted partner. But do I deserve him?

My list is a representation of the kinds of flaws men hide from women on first or second dates. It puts the blame on the men. To use my tattoo curse as a divining rod is to shift my gaze outward. It doesn't present the complete picture. I have flaws, too. What would my announcer dude say about me?

Flaky, unreliable, but kind.
Willing to ignore the truth in front of her.
Puts too much stake in being unique.

Yesterday, I gave Griffin—and myself, while I was at it—a pep talk on the importance of being seen for who you are. I can't say whether it offered him comfort, because he beat a fast retreat to end our text exchange. It definitely sounds like a load of drivel to me today. I don't want to be seen for who I am.

My tattoo curse is the worst. Like Eve, my eyes have opened, and I've been banished from my happy place. I'd give anything for a healthy dose of oblivion. Or a conversation with a friend who totally gets my current state of mind.

CHAPTER 44
GRIFFIN

There's nothing better than a blank document to remind a writer of the myriad alternative tasks he could be tackling. No one would fault me for updating my story bible before I write the next chapter. And it's crucial I reread the last two chapters I wrote to ensure continuity. It's more difficult for me to justify rubbing my eraser over poorly erased entries in my date book as a necessary step for preparing to write. I'm sure the disorder of the loose sheets of paper in my document holder on my desk isn't directly linked to my creative process. I straighten them anyway and then consider putting in a load of laundry.

This isn't writer's block; it's a less severe affliction related somewhat to not having a clear picture of exactly where my protagonist needs to be both physically and mentally at the start of the next scene.

You and me both, Talib.

I'm at my desk in my apartment, alone and pretending to be a writer. Isn't this where I'm supposed to be?

I'm where I was before Daphne summoned me to LA. Before Mallory appeared on my phone. Before Anja burst into my imagination. Still, I wonder whether the alone part had previously given me more grief than I would have admitted. I wouldn't have opened my big mouth and blabbered on to Curly, my tattoo artist, about wanting to connect to women if I didn't hope to find a woman who could see past my scars.

I pat the black bandage still stretched across my forearm. Tomorrow is the big reveal. I'd love to rip the bandage from my arm today and reclaim my earlier state of mind, but the intense woman with blond and pink hair put the fear of god in me when she read me the aftercare instructions.

By Tuesday, things will return to normal. My tattoo will have healed. And by then, I will have visited the nursing home and hopefully solved the mystery. I can call Anja tomorrow and put her and the chaotic limbo of recent days behind me.

Again, I stare at my blank screen. *Two thousand words, Griffin. Half your daily output. Put a few words on the page, and then you can head over to the nursing home.*

My phone rings, and I'm unreasonably excited to have another excuse to ditch work.

"Hello?"

"Oh, good. You answered quickly. I didn't wake you."

I bash my head with my fist. I answered the call before I realized it was from Anja.

"Nope. Been awake for hours."

"Bear with me, because I'm walking and talking. City life might want to say hello."

"No problem. What's up?"

"Our conversation ended abruptly yesterday. I never told you what I'd do if I learned I was going to die tomorrow. And then I wondered whether you'd want to hear it. Right before you signed off, I had painted a vivid mental picture of me resembling a mythical, ungrounded waif. I understand if it was off-putting."

My head sinks. I was so caught up in my own insecurity that I hadn't considered how my actions would impact Anja.

"Quite the opposite. Not only are you not the reason I ended our conversation, but you are also perhaps the most grounded person I've ever met. I'm sorry to have given you the wrong impression. I should have stuck around and asked you to describe your last day alive."

Her speaking pace quickens, and her voice rises in pitch. "Yesterday, I was picturing the way kids tug on a parent's sleeve because they think they have something they have to show them. Of course, they don't; they're just spoiling for attention. Anyway, once they have their parent's attention, they invent, like, the lamest thing ever, executing an awkward, unimpressive spin or what have you. I'd love to run up to strangers, tug on their sleeves, and offer them something beautiful and ephemeral in order to ensure I don't take everything I love with me to my grave. But saying it out loud, I realize it sounds weird."

How is it such a woman thought to call *me* to share her beautiful, ephemeral gift?

I say, "Not to me. I'd love to hear an example."

"I'm approaching an underpass below a busy highway right now. It's both the setting for a gift and a warning things might get squirrelly when I'm in the thick of the noise. Can you hear me?"

"Well enough. Keep going."

"Right. Most people walking the same route I'm on will notice the roads, the chain-link fence, the cars. They'll shrink from the roar of the highway above them. Beyond the underpass, they might notice the trees lining the street, but the trees are incongruous and easy to dismiss. So, my gift might be to point to a bird on a branch of a tree or to the small stuffed lizard on the dash of a car parked on the side of the road. I live for tiny details that put a little zip in my step or banish a gloomy thought. If I can remind people to see beyond the darkness or notice the invisible delights around them, I'd say I had lived a life worth living."

My body buzzes with a jolt of electricity. I want Anja to show me her world. Since writing ain't happening, I plan to head to the nursing home once we've ended our conversation. Should I find our man at the nursing home, I'll need to put on my big boy pants and arrange for her to meet León Roca. And perhaps to meet me, although it will take more strength than I currently have to prepare myself for the meeting. I need to find it, because I suspect the reward could be greater than the risk.

"Wow. Puts my plan to eat, drink, and read in solitude on my last day to shame."

"You hadn't mentioned the solitude part yesterday."

"I'm assuming the current conditions will continue for a while."

"It sounds like you've allowed your ex to speak on your behalf. Get her out of your system, and once you have, you'll find your barbecue-loving, Jules Verne-reading, whisky-sipping companion for the end times."

I want to build a wall against the tidal wave of desire flooding me while I imagine sharing my favorite things with Anja. "On that note—"

"I did it again. I called you because I was having a dark moment and needed to regain my perspective. You have a gift for helping me navigate life's challenges. But I suspect I cured my blues by transferring them to you."

I shrug, not that she can see me. "You didn't send them to me. I'm typically in a bluesy state, but you need to understand you are not part of it."

Not in a way I could explain to her.

"You promise?"

"Cross my heart and hope to die."

"Perfect. I'll send an overnight delivery from my favorite barbecue restaurant because I'm the sort who needs to prove she's right, even to a dying man."

I laugh. "It would be worth sampling yours simply to confirm I had been right in my choice of which is the best barbecue restaurant all along."

"So long as you're honest with yourself on your deathbed, I would respect your preference. Hey, I hate to do this, but I've completed the walking part of my day, which means I have to stop talking and attend to my afternoon plans."

"Don't let me keep you. Speaking of plans, I have an interview with a candidate for the position of missing violinist this afternoon. I'll brief you once I have an answer."

"You have made my day! Give Señor Roca my best!"

"Absolutely. I'm glad you called."

"Me, too."

I curse myself for holding onto the smile she has left me with while I prepare to leave for the nursing home.

CHAPTER 45
ANJA

"¡Hola, chica! You couldn't stay away from us, could you?" Maria asks.

I plant my elbow on the front desk of the nursing home. "The next available room, I'm snatching it and moving in. The gang here has a busier activities schedule than me. I want in on chair aerobics and Wednesday movie matinees."

"Don't forget Sunday afternoon concerts. You'll have a mutiny on your hands if you and your guitar don't get on stage quick."

"I can't possibly be late. I left home early today." And walked at a dreamy pace while talking with Griffin. It got late fast. "I swear time plays dirty tricks on me. Catch you on the flip side."

I swing my guitar case to increase my momentum. Maria wasn't joking. A full house awaits me in the dining room.

I enter the room and tap my wrist where a watch should be. "You guys are early; the singalong doesn't begin for another hour."

"It should have started three minutes ago. Buy a watch, wouldya?" a raspy voice calls to me.

"Ooh, Mr. Cohn! Are you in a rush to get to a hot date after we're done?"

"Not unless you've decided to give me a chance."

"I'd only let you down. You deserve a woman who can keep to a schedule."

"I'd take a woman who can carry a tune. You can make it up to me for being late and rebuffing my overtures by playing *By the Light of the Silvery Moon* first."

I pump my fist twice on my chest and point to Mr. Cohn. "I got you, brother."

My guitar is a twangy mess of out of tune strings. I turn the pegs quickly to prevent the energy in the room from dipping. Without Griffin's help, I'm not sure I would have had the enthusiasm I need to share with my peeps.

I strum a C chord. "Close enough for jazz. Now, the lyrics to my first song are a tad racy. If you're not comfortable singing 'I'd like to spoon,' might I suggest replacing *spoon* with *fork*?" I frown and glance upward, pretending to study my last sentence. "Oof! That's dirtier than the original. Shame on me. This is a family show. We'll stick with *spoon*, folks. And-a-one, and-a-two…"

Most in the room lift their voices to croon and spoon with me. Mr. Lowenstein is on the end of the second row. His spine and neck curl, bending his head nearly into his lap. My music doesn't exist to him. Perhaps once I've sated the crowd with a handful of rowdier tunes, I'll revisit my set from Tuesday. He connected to a piece I had played.

I can't think of song titles while playing another tune, though. You start out singing *Put on a Happy Face* and if you're not careful, it turns into the title song from *Cabaret*. Gray skies certainly can't clear up when you're sitting alone in a room.

Wait. The genius switch switches to the *on* position.

"Mrs. Perlmutter, I could use your help."

She presses on the arms of her chair to stand and patters to my side. "Can we sing *Mairzy Doats?*"

"That's my question for you. I seem to have forgotten how it goes. I'll play the introduction. Could I ask you to lead us in a couple of choruses?"

Her cheeks grow pink, and her blue eyes glisten. "I think I can."

"Then take it away, my friend!" I play a two-bar intro in D and leave her and the crowd to sing it a cappella while I wrack my brain for the tune that sparked Mr. Lowenstein's interest.

I ghost fingering patterns in front of my strings, recreating the scene from Tuesday. People weren't singing with me. Must have been an unfamiliar song. Or I wasn't singing, either. Was it *El Choclo?* I could give it a try. First, I'll lead them in a lively song to distance ourselves from the train wreck that has become of *Mairzy Doats.* Can't segue straight into a demonstration of my decidedly limited finger plucking stylings from their atonal caterwauling.

"And a round of applause for Mrs. Perlmutter! Now return to your seat before Mrs. Ellis turns it into a footstool. My best friend is a near perfect match for my next ditty. Perhaps she's an inch shorter, and her eyes are gray rather than blue, but I recently learned she went missing on me for a week. And, no surprise, her disappearance involved some wooing and cooing. Let's give it up for Violet and sing *Five-Foot-Two, Eyes of Blue.*"

I sweep my gaze through the crowd, landing on Mr. Lowenstein every few bars, but he is not in the moment with us. With a subtle push of the tempo, I bring us to the end sooner rather than later.

"I'm giving your vocal cords a rest with my next selection. It's a repeat from Tuesday, but I believe it was a favorite of Mr. Lowenstein's. Let's go south of the border to Buenos Aires for a tango. Everybody have a rose in their teeth?"

Here's hoping my fingers remember the tune since I haven't played it in days. I establish my tango groove and dig in, staring at the strings. I sense movement before I can raise my head. In between verses, I play a four-measure interlude. Mr. L.'s left hand is doing its turtle-on-its-back routine, his hand resting on the arm of his wheelchair with his palm in the air. His fingers twitch, and his eyes lock onto mine. A shiver races along my spine when I sense a second pair of eyes boring into me.

I shift my attention to a man who leans against the doorframe on the side of the room, a few rows behind Mr. Lowenstein. Our eyes lock on each other for a split second, forcing his face into a mask of terror.

CHAPTER 46
GRIFFIN

The walk to the nursing home restores my sense of normalcy. I'm practiced in following Anja's advice to notice details, at least while passing the apartment on 7th Street, with its riot of colors in the windows and random collection of toys in its window boxes. Glancing at it today is a comforting tic, something familiar and expected coming through for me.

The wooded stretches of Newark and Palisades Avenues are also favorite landmarks along the walk. Despite the graffiti-covered railroad and New Jersey Turnpike bridges in the background, the trees have the power to whisk me away from the somewhat oppressive qualities of New Jersey's second largest city into momentary tranquility. I peer over the fence into the woods for a last breath of nature. To look over the bridge a block in front of me would offer a view of the clogged roadway leading to the Holland Tunnel.

The nursing home is less than half a mile further. I reach it a few minutes later. Strands of toilet paper are strung around a branch in a tree in front of the nursing home in a small, starlike blob. Were it a larger installation, I'd be angry with the vandal who hid the tiny shred of nature outside the windows of residents on this side of the three-story building. But the white fluttering in the light breeze isn't ugly. I hope someone with a view of it sees art in the tree, not litter.

I approach the reception desk inside and speak to the woman behind it. "Hi, I'm Griffin Hull. I believe Steven Lefkovitz called to let you know I would be visiting his father-in-law?"

"Ah, yes. So nice of you to visit him. He is in the dining room, straight ahead, listening to the music. You can wait by the door. I'll send an aide in to bring him to his room."

"Thank you."

Strains of a song from the turn of the last century bleed into the lobby. A boisterous, tonality-challenged crowd sings along with the guitar. I inch my way toward the room, not quite ready to take it on full blast. The music changes to a tango for guitar solo. I close my eyes with a contented grin. If I believed in signs and magical powers, I'd swear the tune was more than a coincidence. But a random song can't make my assumption I'll meet León Roca today become true.

I hold onto the doorframe, letting my eyes drift across the rows of people who watch the guitarist while keeping the left side of my face facing the doorframe. Many have fallen under the spell of the music, moving their heads, hands, or feet along with the rhythm, me included. My fingers begin to drum against the painted wood trim without my permission.

The guitarist hunches over her instrument, studying the dance of her fingers on the strings. Waves of long, pale blond hair crest her shoulder, coming dangerously close to the action. She raises her head to glance at her audience.

A glow radiates from her face, which is a moon of softness and goodwill. A second later, her eyes meet mine. I freeze. I recognize her. She is the woman who sat across from me at the tattoo parlor.

I'm a weak fool to let a beautiful woman who is busy doing things that have nothing to do with me terrorize me. But I'm not ready to deal with the existence of a woman I had wished I could meet. I take a step backward, removing her from my view while I wait for the aide.

CHAPTER 57
ANJA

I pluck a few horrifically wrong notes in response to the horrified expression exploding from the right side of the face of the man clutching the doorframe. *Focus, Anja!* To save myself, I insert a multi-measure vamp while I regain my composure and study the dude during the couple of seconds he stares at me.

He's around my age and has an adorable crop of curly, light brown hair piled atop his head. I'm a sucker for guys in round tortoiseshell glasses, especially on the faces of men with lanky bodies. Either we have met before or he isn't interested in me because my announcer buddy remains quiet.

Did we date? Did I hurt him?

I'm pretty sure I don't recognize him. Before I can know for certain, he disappears.

Think about Mr. Lowenstein. You chose to play El Choclo *for him.*

I'm determined to conquer verse two. I take a surreptitious glance at Mr. L. He's still with me. If he weren't, I'd be this close to ditching my guitar and running after the mysterious stranger. He had a pull on me, and I need to know why.

Play the chorus, Madame Distracto. Now is not the time for boys.

I return to tangoing. An aide approaches Mr. Lowenstein's chair. *You notice him responding to the music, don't you? How cool is it for him to be alert?* The aide unlocks the wheels on his chair. *Leave him alone.* She doesn't respond to my telepathy.

The handles firmly in her grip, she makes a U-turn with him and pushes him toward the door.

No! Bring him back!

Instead, like the horrified stranger, he slips out of view.

CHAPTER 48
GRIFFIN

Jacob's head swivels to the left, homing in on the open door the farther away from the concert we take him.

"He seems to enjoy the music," I say.

"She plays for us every week. He'll hear her again. It's a special day for Mr. Lowenstein to have a visitor."

The three of us enter the elevator. The doors close, cutting us off from the music. Mr. Lowenstein's head droops until his chin nearly rests on his sternum.

On the third floor, the aide wheels him into a room with a view of the toilet paper star. She backs the chair into the space between the bed and the wall dividing his room from the hallway. His roommate's bed is closest to the window.

"Mr. Lowenstein, can I get anything for you?" the aide asks. He is unresponsive. To me, she says, "He never speaks. It is rare he's aware we're here, but I'm sure in his own way he'll enjoy having a visitor. He likes to hold hands. I hope the two of you have a pleasant visit." She smiles broadly and exits the room.

I slide a blue vinyl-covered armchair opposite him, its feet screeching against the linoleum tiled floor. "Mr.

Lowenstein, my name is Griffin Hull. I have been searching for a man, and after speaking with your son-in-law Steven, I wanted to meet you to determine whether you are the man I am searching for."

He is immobile except for his mouth, which he works into a frown, pressing and releasing his lower lip against the upper.

Do I address him as León Roca? The Spanish name translates into lion rock. So does Lowenstein. And the name he used during his brief solo career, Lionel Jacobs, attaches his first name to another form of the word lion. How could the man before me not be my missing violinist?

Speaking to him won't accomplish anything. I had witnessed how alert he was to the music downstairs. I pull out my phone and search for the Canaro y Roca album that first captured my attention. It needs to be the second track, Verano Porteño, by Astor Piazzolla.

I position the phone in my lap, pointing it at him. Arminda Canaro establishes the stomping rhythm on the bandoneon. León Roca plucks along with her before the two sweep together into the melody in messy, passionate strokes. Mr. Lowenstein raises his head. The fingers on his left hand imitate the violin's patterns. His frown melts into the slightest of smiles. His eyes find mine.

"Is this you playing the violin? Are you León Roca?"

His grin widens until the tips of yellowed, crooked teeth crest his lips. He grunts, his voice raspy and weak.

My hand is too shaky to hold the phone. I place it atop his bed. "I have learned a great deal about you, Mr. Lowenstein. Let me show you the photographs and press clippings I've brought."

I reach into my bag for the Manila envelope. I tease the stack of pages from the envelope and lay them in his lap. After lowering the volume on the phone, I stand beside his chair, hunched over to reach the papers and photos.

One by one, I lift them in front of his face. His hands touch the bottom edges. He studies each photo and newspaper clipping. Who knows what he can see through his ancient, watery eyes? But he remains engaged. He finds meaning in each item. I hold my favorite photo before him, an action shot of the duo. His fingers trace Ms. Canaro's hair.

"She is beautiful. The two of you are beautiful together. Thank you for your music."

His hands fall into his lap, but his smile lingers. With a gentle tug, I extract the pile of documents and place them into the envelope. I set it on his nightstand, but think the better of it, returning it to my bag. I should frame a few of the memories to keep them safely accessible to Mr. Lowenstein.

"Let me tell you how I found you. I tracked you to your early solo career under the management of Apollo Artists. Do you remember Clive Samuels? He made you change your name. Was it your idea to become Lionel Jacobs to keep your name close to its original? And then you had to reinvent yourself as an Argentinian when you formed your duo with Arminda Canaro. You sacrificed both your voice and your name for the sake of music. I bet not many people today know who the real León Roca is."

He has a mischievous glint in his eye. He and I might be the only two people in on his secret. I can't keep it to myself. Anja needs to hear the news.

"I had a lot of assistance in finding you, starting with a woman at Apollo Artists. The story of our visit will make her day, I'm sure. Perhaps she can meet you soon. I also spoke with Edith, Miss DeLay's assistant at Juilliard. Do you remember her?"

He grunts again.

"And finally, I found you in the obituary for your wife. I'm so sorry for your loss. Your son-in-law Steven arranged for me to meet you today. You have led an amazing life. I will ensure the people who care for you know your story. We'll hang pictures in your room and have them play your music. And I will visit you often. We're neighbors."

Mr. Lowenstein's eyes have lost their sparkle. Gravity is winning the fight with his body, which slumps in his chair like a mudslide.

"It has been an exciting afternoon for you. I'll leave you to enjoy a rest. But Mr. Lowenstein or León Roca, however you want to be remembered, you will be."

I wrap my palms around his hands and give them a squeeze. While I had his attention, I didn't need anyone else to share the moment. But now, as I return to the life I had escaped during the visit, I'm jumpy and untethered. I should call Anja and tell her the news right away. Unfortunately, I doubt my body can handle anyone else's energy.

MONDAY

CHAPTER 49
ANJA

"Eleven and a half more hours, and you are history!" I pound my fists toward the sky when I step onto the sidewalk in front of my house on Monday morning. I'm not raging because we're in danger of the sky falling tonight. What I mean is that at eight tonight, I can ditch my nuisance curse announcer.

He has been of absolutely no use to me the entire week. What is the point of making a wish (unbeknownst to you, but still...) on magical tattoo ink if you wind up with nothing to show for it?

I will lament never finding the owner of the unknown voice I heard at the tattoo gallery until the end of time, no doubt. But every other announcement has served no purpose. I would have discovered barbecue-loving Blake from Wednesday wasn't into me soon enough. Well, there is one other exception: Mr. Lowenstein talked to me, albeit it telepathically. That said, I had understood his thoughts by reading his body language.

I appreciate the way my narrator *could* have helped me, and lord knows, I'd be dancing for joy had he accomplished what I needed him to accomplish. Perhaps I stand an outside chance of striking gold before tonight. On the way to work, I halfheartedly give meeting my next boyfriend the old college try, making eye contact with every man within fifteen feet of me. I can practically see my magical dude rolling up his sleeves before grabbing a mic for his last hurrah.

Give me your best, Mr. Announcer!

"He helps himself to money he finds in his dates' wallets."

"He'd rather be playing video games."

"His wandering eye achieves over 10,000 steps daily."

Yeah, I won't miss the warning labels.

I lower my head as I exit the light rail and race toward my office without the accompaniment of a highlight reel of humanity's flaws. It's a drag to be walking into Apollo Artists after only one day off, but having discovered a sweet spot between what Mrs. Cuthbert wants and how I'd recommend we proceed, I'm ready to tackle whatever she throws at me. I have a much better chance of succeeding at my job than in love. Best to go with the sure thing.

Alejandro arrives at his desk, catty-corner from mine. He glances at his watch and then at me. "Excuse me? Have we met?"

I wave. "Hi, I'm Anja, and I came to work five minutes early."

He shakes his hands at the sides of his head in a panicked version of jazz hands. "It's like I don't even know you anymore."

"We have an email blast going out at nine. I want to watch the magic of the ever-climbing open rates and clicks."

"Perhaps I'm in the wrong workplace. Did you say we sent a mailing via email?"

"The boss and I determined on Saturday it would be the ideal way to fix the problem of having omitted the Stella Étoile Quartet from our snail mail newsletter."

"Will wonders ever cease?"

"Did I mention she chose the version I wrote in my voice, not hers? Now, please leave me alone, because I am a busy woman."

He pushes his hands toward me, full-on freaking out. "Holy smokes, the situation is more serious than I had imagined. When have you ever abandoned me mid-conversation to work?"

He's not wrong about me. Not for the first time, I'm grateful my curse wasn't a perpetual broadcast of my true nature. I am more than I appear to be. I'd better start acting like it.

CHAPTER 50
GRIFFIN

I've dragged my heels long enough. I need to report my news to Anja. *She is not—and will never be—your girlfriend, Griffin. Don't treat her as anything but a colleague.* It's not her fault she entered my life in the week where I finally had game with women, at least through my phone. I'm to blame for falling for her.

Tell her the news and be done with her already!

I could send her a text…

Stop being a wimp!

With a sigh, I click on her name to connect the call. She answers immediately. I say, "Hey, Anja. I can call back if you're busy."

"I'm never too busy. What's up?"

"I've found León Roca."

She gasps. "That is huge. Congratulations!"

"He's a resident at a nursing home. Um… What was the name? Oh, yes. Riverside Jewish Care Center."

"In Jersey City?"

"Yeah. You've heard of it?"

"I was at the center yesterday. I volunteer two or three days a week. More like I volunteer the sweet, captive audience to endure me squawking along with my amateur-level guitar playing."

My breathing becomes shallow. *Paper bags, paper bags.* I rustle through the nearest closet to hunt for one but come up empty. My fingertips are tingling, and I doubt I will remain conscious for much longer. I tear two sheets of paper towel from the roll, slap them over my mouth, and force myself to inhale to the bottom of my lungs.

"Griffin? You have a bad connection. Are you there?"

I stab the red button to end the call and frantically search for a clock emoji to text her. The whoosh of the message leaving my phone reminds me to regulate my breath. I shuffle over to the couch and let gravity suck me downward. The leatherette cushion squeaks and crunches under my weight.

I press my palms on my chest to slow my breath. That was Anja playing the tango yesterday? The cognitive dissonance of the random ways my life keeps intersecting with hers fights with my efforts to regain a healthy heart and respiration rate.

Were I to write the same string of coincidences into a novel, my readers would flay me in their reviews for the lack of plausibility. It reeks of qualities beyond the known world. And I don't do occult. There must be a different explanation.

Once I've chugged a glass of water, I dial Anja again. "Sorry. I had to tend to something."

"I didn't mind. Well, except for the part about you leaving me to freak out on my own, wondering who our secret tango violinist could be. I have a hunch, though."

"Do you want to guess?" I ask.

"I would. I'm thinking of a man who appears to be a fan of a particular tango I recently added to my repertoire. Is it Mr. Lowenstein?"

My body can't handle my impulse to rush in with the full story. I carve a slower path toward the reveal. "Do you know what the translation of Lowenstein is?"

"A short, scrapheap of a reanimated human?"

I pull the phone from my ear to avoid laughing loudly in hers. "Stein means stone in German. And the Spanish word for stone is Roca."

"No! Does Lowen mean lion?"

"It does. And his first name, Jacob, became his last name during his solo career. The Jacob Lowenstein you've met is hardly the only Jacob Lowenstein in the US, but I had a hunch. You mentioned he responded when you played a tango for him. Why did you choose the piece?"

"It was random, as is the case with many things in my life. A few weeks ago, I tasked myself to learn to play melodies along with the accompaniment. I intended to select a classical piece, but *El Choclo* was the shiny object in the room. I debuted it last Tuesday. While I played the piece, Mr. Lowenstein emerged from his fog. Oh! That's what he was doing with his left hand. He was playing the violin with me. I wish I had made the connection between the lost old man I knew and the lost old man we were looking for. No matter. You found him. Since I'm in Jersey City and you're in California, it makes sense for me to visit him. Should I?"

"I'm home from my trip to LA. Sorry I confused you regarding my whereabouts. I never changed my phone number after I moved to New Jersey. Truth is, I went to visit him yesterday."

"I wish I had known you were there. I would have coordinated my visit."

"Uh, no worries. You were busy entertaining the crowd."

"Wait. You're the reason they wheeled Mr. Lowenstein out of the singalong." I hear humming on the other end. "You were standing in the doorway with a horrified expression on your face. I told you: I'm an amateur guitarist and volunteer. Not cool to dis my guitar stylings."

"What? You worried I was judging your playing? Oh, gosh, I'm so sorry. You were fantastic, and the residents clearly loved your performance. I… No. Hah. I've been cagey with you and won't be breaking my streak now, but the thing is, I prefer to exist sight unseen. It's why I love being an author."

"Does being in public terrify you?"

"No. Making connections does. I recognized you, and in an instant, I became visible."

"You knew I was me? I had wondered whether we had met before, but I drew a blank. Now I'm really mad at you for not introducing yourself."

"I didn't know you were my sleuthing partner until a few minutes ago. The revelation of you having been at the nursing home yesterday knocked me for a loop. There are too many coincidences, Anja. And I'm not comfortable explaining them to you."

Air whistles against her lips while she inhales. "Where did we first meet, Griffin?" Her tone has become steely.

"At Inklyn, a week ago. We didn't meet, but we sat across from each other."

"Hmm. Did your tattooist use Mystic Mate ink?"

"I don't remember the name, but your tattoo artist had a conniption fit over the importance of following the aftercare instructions. I've done everything she told me to do, but the instructions never made sense to me. No matter. The bandage comes off tonight."

"I have one last question, and you need to take me dead seriously. Did you wish for anything?"

Did I what?

CHAPTER 51
ANJA

Griffin is breaking my twenty-minute-long streak of behaving like a focused, dedicated employee. It takes everything I have not to fly around the office in a tizzy in response to the information dump he has laid on me. I have so much more ground to cover with him, it's not funny. Unfortunately, because the conversation doesn't relate to my job, it will have to wait while I prove my worth to Apollo Artists.

I say, "Here. Let me keep you company in the cagey realm. We need to continue our tattoo ink conversation, but I can't delve into it right now. My tattoo unveiling is at eight tonight. Yours is earlier. What time did they put on the bandage?"

"Oh, maybe seven, seven-fifteen?"

"Right. We have ourselves a two-parter. Can I buy you a platter of the world's finest smoked meat tonight to celebrate the release of our tattoos and the discovery of our violinist's identity?"

"This again? I will defend Hamilton Pork to the end of days, so if you dare force me to—"

218

"Griffin, Griffin, Griffin. Relax, would you? I, too, am a Hamilton Pork devotee. We should have investigated our barbecue loyalties days ago." The silence on his end rattles my nerves. "Did I lose you again?"

"No, still here. Do you, by chance, live on 7th Street?"

"Not by chance. On purpose."

"Do you have dead plants and toys in your window boxes?"

"Live plants don't mix with my Día de Muertos mask. I have to maintain the theme. Let me guess: you live across the street from me, and my black thumb offends you."

"You have more plants—dead or alive—than me. I'm not one to judge. And no, I'm around the corner from you, on Monmouth."

"Howdy, neighbor!"

He sighs, which isn't an encouraging way to greet a long-lost stranger. "There is some weirdness afoot. But I don't want to get into it," he says.

I am now certain he made a wish while under the tattoo gun, and I am dying to know what it was. Can't blame the guy for not wanting to unload a whale of a tale on me, though. He couldn't reasonably expect for me to believe him.

I say, "Trust me: the past week has been a doozy for me, too. A friend clued me in to the reason nothing has made sense. The story is decidedly not fit for the office. Let's circle back to my suggestion of gathering over barbecue tonight."

"I appreciate the offer, but I'll take a rain check."

"I don't accept rain checks. Especially on sunny days."

"Look, Anja, I'm not good with people."

"I beg to differ. The highlight of my week was talking and texting with you. The skill level you need to survive tonight is at a one. First, you'll have a pile of tasty meat in which you can seek comfort. And second, I am never at a loss for words. Should you need to be an introvert, I'll cover you, which is especially easy. Since our lives have billions of parallels, we won't run out of topics to discuss. You don't have to try to be anything with me. Just be you."

"Being me still feels raw at the moment."

"I believe brisket is a known cure for your affliction."

He grows quiet again. I interpret it to be a promising sign.

"Okay, but here are my rules. We'll meet at seven. By then, I'll have claimed a table and will have ordered my meal for takeout. It's my choice whether I stay. My departure might be abrupt. Should I decide to leave, you will not be able to reverse my decision. Do you agree with my conditions?"

"I respect your conditions. See you at seven."

"Okay."

I shove my phone to the side of my desk. It has brought way too many distractions into my day. But they're exciting distractions.

Time to make Apollo Artists a priority in my life. I roll my chair in a semicircle to face Alejandro. Before I embark on today's tasks, I need to tie up a loose end.

"Thanks to your suggestion that I read the autobiography, we found our missing violinist. Remember the guy Clive Samuels forced to change his name when we represented him around 1950? He chose Lionel Jacobs because his original name was too ethnic for the heart of America to embrace?"

He screws up his face. "Our founder's prejudices have bothered me ever since. It isn't a brand I'm proud to represent."

"Preach. The story is Lionel Jacobs became León Roca when he formed a duo with an Argentinian piano player. And now he's living under his own name, Jacob Lowenstein, across the street from Christ Hospital at the nursing home where I volunteer. How weird is that?"

"You have the perfect story for your next newsletter. Speaking of which, I've received two emails this morning about Stella Étoile. Did you embed the booking department's email in the photo?"

"Why, yes. Quick. We have to tell Mrs. Cuthbert."

I have never voluntarily ventured into her office, but she needs to hear the news this second. She sits at her desk, pen in hand, editing a document placed in the center of an otherwise clutter-free green blotter atop her antique desk. I rap on the doorframe. "Um, Mrs. Cuthbert? Do you have a second?"

She readjusts her glasses. "What is it, dear?"

I beckon for Alejandro to follow me into her office. I can't blame him for taking hesitant steps. He also has a history of scary summonses into her lair.

"Alejandro is receiving inquiries about Stella Étoile, based on our electronic newsletter."

"He is? And you can tell this how?"

He steps forward. "Two colleges in Ohio and Indiana have contacted us since receiving the mailing. Anja worked her magic so that when a recipient clicks on a picture of the quartet, it triggers their email server to create a blank email with the booking department's address in the 'to' field and 'Please contact me regarding the Stella Étoile Quartet' in the subject line."

His response inspires her to remove her glasses and stare at him, mouth agape. "I understood next to nothing about what you've told me, but so long as Anja does, I'll assume everything is working properly. All that matters to me is her newsletter generated interest. Well done, Anja. And Alejandro, put together a midwest tour for the quartet for next season. Once you have confirmed dates with the two venues that you're in contact with, reach out to others to build around the dates." She claps her hands. "Oh, this is wonderful. We should send more newsletters on the computer. And I'd like you to take a second look at a few of our clients' materials with an eye on potential updates. I'll compile a list. You might have landed on the proper tone for us to use in certain cases; for instance, artists whose repertoire expands beyond the strictly classical realm might benefit from your modern approach."

I grasp my right thumb with my left hand and raise my shoulders toward my ears. I'm not accustomed to her deeming my efforts worth repeating. Especially when I did everything the opposite of how she had wanted me to. "Once you've decided who you want to promote, I will create mailings for you to approve."

"I will have a list for you soon. Thank you for putting your plan in motion. Alejandro, you'll keep me abreast of your progress?"

"Absolutely."

"That will do."

We exit her office, me very nearly pulling another sniveling, servile maneuver by backing away and bowing. This day definitely deserves to be feted with a visit to Hamilton Pork.

CHAPTER 52
GRIFFIN

I swear I have lost my mind. Nothing makes sense. I pace around my apartment, lost in a frenzied fog. My skin is clammy, and my mouth is dry. I have a massive case of fight or flight, but the cause doesn't merit my reaction. Either I am overreacting, or I am missing a crucial piece of information, which my body is preparing to receive in advance.

An examination of the collision of the multiple Anja-related events could lead to the source of this mess. Taken individually, each event sounds normal. Plausible, even.

Inklyn is a well-reviewed, popular tattoo gallery one mile from our apartments. It is not unrealistic for the two of us to have landed in chairs opposite each other.

J. Adams and Daughter handles the publicity needs for clients in multiple fields, including classical music. For them to have signed a client managed by Apollo Artists again is logical. For an aspiring screenwriter like I had been once upon a time, the publicity firm was a fine place to begin my career. And Anja, a music lover, belongs in her job.

Running into her at the nursing home is unusual only because of our prior connections. She has such a gift, such a rapport with the residents. It's natural to have discovered her volunteering at a local senior care facility.

The devil is in the repetition. Why did our lives continuously intersect throughout the week? I don't go in for the concept of predestination. My mind refuses to believe Anja and I were meant to meet. It was by chance we connected at Inklyn a week ago, a theory proven by how normal everything was until then.

Daphne had made her arrangements to drag me to LA before the tattoo. She had been hinting for months I was beyond overdue for a visit. My conniving sister orchestrated Mallory's reappearance into my life. It also preceded my tattoo. Things didn't take a turn toward weird until after the tattoo.

Why did Anja ask me whether I had made a wish? Did she make one? And is she under the illusion that somehow magical tattoo ink made her wish come true? No way *I* could have been her wish.

I had joked with Curly about wanting to establish better connections with women, perhaps outside the dating context. And out of sight. If I had even used the word *wish*, I didn't mean it like a fervent prayer I believed would be answered.

No, the direction in which I'm taking my hypothesis is ridiculous.

What is eating me alive is having to sit across the table from Anja tonight. I don't need to turn toward sorcery to explain my hyperventilated behavior. A woman I find attractive, with whom I connect on an indescribable, life-affirming level, wants to eat dinner with me at my favorite restaurant. Once she has a closeup view of my scars, she will vanish from my life. We've found León Roca. Nothing binds her to me from now on.

I almost crave having her reject me. The pain will give me the clean cut I need. It worked with Mallory, didn't it?

I slide my phone in front of me on the kitchen counter. My pointer drifts along the list of contacts in my text folder until I land on Mallory's. I reread the text she sent on Saturday morning. It didn't come from a woman who had expected a romantic reconciliation. She hoped to spend an hour or two with the guy she had been texting, not with the guy she had dated years ago.

She didn't reject me because of my face. The rejection took place five years ago when she dumped me. On Friday night, she was insensitive, perhaps, but nothing she did should have left me with another scar. I put her in a position to judge me without sharing the rules with her.

The dread infesting my gut in anticipation of meeting Anja tonight comes from the same source. She and I have established a strong connection. I have no idea what it means to her. To expect her to rewrite the outcome of our myriad encounters because I want her to see past my scar is to set her up to fail. She will see me the way she sees me. If her plan is to celebrate our sleuthing and be tattoo buddies, my face won't matter to her.

Sure, she might cringe, and that's never fun to witness. I need to stick to a survival plan: expect nothing from her. I'm meeting a colleague. We might have enjoyed our collaboration, but tonight presents us with a logical ending. My bag of barbecue and I will head home, and I'll have lost nothing.

Provided I can convince myself that a woman whose digital companionship feels like home is nothing.

CHAPTER 53
ANJA

My belly flutters like a hummingbird with a massive sugar rush. Or a flock of butterflies drunk on nectar. Perhaps the little guy on my ankle migrated into my torso. I stand in front of my bathroom mirror and run my fingers through my long, blond hair, fluffing it up after its day of behaving itself in a corporate-adjacent updo. I don't know; maybe I should return it to its restrictive rubber band and reclaim the dark blue sweater and brown trousers I discarded in favor of a wrap dress featuring a lemon print. My outfit screams date. It shouldn't.

But I don't have time to change. I have seven minutes to make the eight-minute walk to Hamilton Pork. My plans of dawdling along Monmouth Street to play "guess which apartment is Griffin's" have to go the way of my hope of finding a spark with him. My neighborhood, its residents, and the occasional voiceover fade in a blur along my frenzied dash. A man who has warned me he might bolt the restaurant for any reason would surely count my tardiness amongst his grievances.

I arrive at the restaurant, breathless. My cheeks must be an off-putting shade of blotchy pink. The likelihood of my wrap dress having come unwrapped under my sweater-coat is high. Leave it to my inability to stick to a schedule to render me less date-ready. I'll take it.

A blast of meat-scented nirvana greets me through the open door. Bad things can't happen in here. The wood-heavy decor, fairy lights, and the general busyness of people preparing, serving, and reveling in all that is barbecue creates a force field against negativity. I scan the room for Griffin.

My fluttering woodland creatures leap from my belly into my chest when I spot him. Light brown curls crest his head, which hovers over the top of his open takeout bag. His fingers emerge from the bag with a clutch of fries. It's a moment of perfect indiscipline. I'd lose respect for him were he able to flee the scene without first diving into the goodness contained within his bag.

I stand a respectful three feet from him. "I believe your entrée is jealous of the fries. It has given its life for your enjoyment and therefore does not cotton to being overlooked in favor of a lowly potato."

He lifts his head. Soulful brown eyes fight with eyelids that implore his gaze to be wary. I want to wrap him in a hug and promise he's safe with me.

"Um, hi," he says.

"Hi, yourself. Before I exhibit my wide range of social niceties, I must inform you I am starving. The question I need to answer is whether to order for here or to go. Oh, and whether I'm taking my meat with soft tacos or a roll. And then there's the pulled pork versus pork belly conundrum. Other than that, I'm totally on top of my dinner plans."

With his head lowered and tilted on its axis to favor his right side, he bites his thumbnail and glances at me over the tops of his tortoiseshell glasses. "Tacos. Pork belly. For here."

"I am in the presence of a master. I bow to you, sir." Since I didn't exceed my quota of servile gestures at the office today, I curtsy before him.

He shrugs and points to the empty chair across from him. I unbutton my coat, taking a quick peek inside first to make sure my bits and pieces aren't spilling out of my dress. With the dress where it should be, I slip my coat from my shoulders and onto the back of the bent cane chair. I check my phone. "Ten minutes left with your bandage. Do you have a eulogy prepared to commend it for its service?"

"It's just a bandage."

"A bandage that has done an important job of protecting your— What is it protecting?"

He unbuttons the right cuff of his French blue button-down shirt. He meticulously folds the cuff in half and rolls the sleeve to his elbow. A black bandage stretches from his wrist to nearly the bend of his arm. "Random black and red blobs." He stares at the bandage, and his fingers fiddle with the rolled part of the sleeve.

I give him the gentlest smile I can muster. Whatever comfort level we had established over the past week hasn't accompanied him to the restaurant. I sort through my memory banks of our conversations, landing on the theme of being seen as more than meets the eye.

Not to be presumptuous, but I wonder what role the scar at the corner of his eye, which drips onto his prominent cheekbone and down to his mouth, played in whatever happened with his ex. I mean, sure, it is there, on his face. But so are a pair of eyes that hold incredible softness and depth within them. His eyelashes are too lush and long to be legal for a person who probably would never glue false eyelashes onto his lids in an attempt to turn wussy blond lashes into fringe with more vavoom had they been his lot in life only to wind up gluing his eye shut. *Not that I would have any familiarity with such a predicament, she says, rolling her eyes to their upper corners.*

He has an award-winning crop of curls he wears long on top and short on the sides. Curls that my fingers itch to pull to their full length before letting them spring into their predestined coils. And he is definitely a huggable size, tall enough and with shoulders wide enough to give me something to hold on to. But he is not broad, which would allow my arms to wrap full around him, to bring him close enough to me until he'd meld into me.

And then we have the matter of his lips. His lower lip has enough fullness to lure me into inappropriate dreams of sucking on it. The upper lip is thin and takes an upward turn on the left side, rendering his mouth into a sneer. Without the kindness in his eyes, I'd worry. Taken together, they make me smile.

Were it not for the appearance of our server, I would not have been able to break my streak of taking surreptitious glances at him to absorb the full picture. I place my order and settle into my seat once we're alone. "You never answered my question about a wish. Did anything change after your tattoo?"

He raises his brow and taunts me by sucking his lower lip. His hesitancy provides an answer that his response cannot support. "Nope."

Where is the man in my phone, the guy who joked and peeled away layers of himself like an artichoke to reveal his tender, sweet heart? "Would you be more comfortable if we parted ways or continued our conversation on our phones?"

"I told you I'm not good with people. But you can stay."

"I'm glad." I glance at my phone again. "It is time for you to reveal your tattoo."

He inhales deeply through his nose, his chest pressing toward me. I lower my eyes to avoid making him more uncomfortable. With a cock of his head and a sniff, he tugs each of the four strips of tape from his skin. The bandage lifts with the fourth.

He rubs his fingers across the ink, which lies vivid against the pale underside of his forearm. I have the sense he has let me drift away into oblivion. I count to thirty before I speak. "Miro?"

He startles, remembering I'm with him. "Yeah."

"Cool. Do you feel different? I had a weird tingling sensation at one point during my tattoo, followed by a dizzy spell." He bites his lower lip, and his eyes retreat to their corners. I wait for him to speak, but he doesn't. "Because of the craziness from this week, and after hearing a story from a friend, I'm expecting a similar experience at my unveiling."

He rubs his forearm. "No. Everything's the same."

I don't believe him. I can't believe him. What happens if my curse doesn't lift after I remove my bandage?

CHAPTER 54
GRIFFIN

et a grip, Griffin! Did Anja shudder? Did she say something rude?

G The truth is, she didn't so much as even swallow hard when we met. I did not witness any hitch or readjustment in her eyes. She smiled with the kind of warmth I had grown to expect to radiate through the phone during our conversations. She saw me, not my scar.

So why have I reverted to the old version of Griffin?

I'm waiting for the warning sign, the reason I should bail on her to protect myself. Yet none is forthcoming. I want to take a sledgehammer to the walls I've built around me, but I lack the strength. She is not Mallory. I suspect I have far more to lose should she reject me.

I rub the tattoo again, half expecting the black and red ink to stand above my arm in relief. The tattooed patches lie flush with my skin, just above the scars. They create the optical illusion of turning the scars into shadows. The meaning behind the injury recedes, too. My arm is me now, better for the scars.

Without a magical tattoo, the scar on my face relies on me behaving differently. No way I'm letting Anja slip away because of my fears. I unroll my sleeve partway before reversing course. I need the tattoo to remind me of the split second of confidence I had after I first unwrapped it.

"All right. I'll bite. What's this about wishes and tattoos?" I ask.

Anja takes a furtive glance around her. "I don't fancy myself a witch or a believer in magic or anything weird. Listen with an open mind, okay?"

My fingertips graze the tattoo, further exciting the tingling sensation that has not quit since I removed the bandage. She hasn't judged me. I owe her the same. "I'm listening."

"Right. I have the lousiest track record of dating men who present very well but who are actually hiding a fatal flaw. It puts me at a tremendous disadvantage because with me, what you see is what you get. Anyhow, while Amelia was tattooing me, I casually wished men came with warning labels the way prescription drugs do in TV commercials. My body tingled like mad, and I grew dizzy. I made eye contact with a man, and the next thing I knew, an announcer's voice informed me of the man's long history of one-night stands. Other unflattering statements flooded my ears, and they haven't ceased. If a man who wants a piece of this…" Her hands sweep along the sides of a torso I've found too enticing to ignore. " … I hear his fatal flaw. And every man has a fatal flaw." She squints. "Well, almost all of them. And I don't hear the voice when I'm with a man I've seen or met before."

I'm more vulnerable than I have been at any moment since Anja approached my table. For a brief instance at Inklyn, our eyes met. Was it before or after her wish? I'm not saying I totally believe her, but I can't help but feel violated by the notion of her hearing a story I didn't agree to share.

"Did you hear anything when we met?"

"That's the thing. The first time I knew I was making eye contact with you was yesterday. Nada. And definitely nothing tonight."

I scan the room. A man at the table across from us is checking out Anja. "What about him?" I indicate the ogler with a tilt of my head.

She takes a breath before shifting her eyes toward him. Her face slides from neutral to disgusted. She turns toward me. "I cannot wait until eight."

"What did he say?"

"I'd rather not repeat it."

I glance over my shoulder. Dude is still staring at Anja. My shoulder jolts, prepping me to punch the simper from the creep's face. "I trust you."

"Regarding the wish?"

"Yeah, that." I meant it more as a blanket statement, but I'm keeping my secrets to myself.

She pulls a dog-eared lavender notebook from her purse. "I've kept a record of the statements. Your warning label should be in here. I never learned who belonged to the first half dozen statements I heard at Inklyn." She pats the notebook. "What should a woman know about you before dating you?"

"You've asked one heck of a loaded question. Forgive me for not jumping in with an answer."

"You're right. I could throw a few words from my journal at you to see what sticks."

"I'm going to hate hearing you say it, aren't I?"

"Provided your greatest wish for your next relationship is backdoor access, yes."

"Dodged a bullet. What else you got?"

"You aren't married, so I'm eliminating that one. Funny?"

"I suppose."

"You are. Honest?"

Am I honest? Hiding from view isn't the most honest of behaviors. "I don't lie to hurt people, but I might withhold the truth to protect myself."

"I respect that. Are you a boob man?" I snort at an embarrassing decibel level. "Too vague. Are boobs more important than the woman to whom they're attached?"

Don't explain your views on the importance of breasts or the interest you're taking in what lies in front of you. That's not the question she asked.

"Not a chance."

"I think I've pegged you." She bites her lip, growing shy. With a swift movement, she closes the notebook and slips it into her purse.

"Not fair. You know my secret. Tell me what the announcer said about me."

"You remember saying you sometimes lie to protect yourself? I plead the fifth."

"Okay." I'm not okay with her response, but I don't want to make her uncomfortable. "You asked whether I had made a wish. I didn't have voices following me around this week. Honestly, nothing I'd identify as magical happened."

"People don't go around making wishes twenty-four-seven. It's entirely plausible you didn't make a wish. In which case, you had a normal tattoo experience."

I haven't stumbled on a logical explanation for why I fell into easy conversations with every woman I was in contact with over the last week. And I have the nagging suspicion I used the "w" word when I mused over the concept of connecting to a woman via text. What else besides magic could explain why Anja is sitting across from me tonight after a week of encouraging me to reveal myself to her over the phone? Did she fall for me the way I had fallen for her?

The server interrupts my train of thought by placing a metal tray with exquisite cuts of pork arranged atop of a piece of butcher paper in front of Anja. I lose her for a moment, not that anyone else wouldn't be doomed to playing second fiddle to a hot platter of smoked pork belly. I look on, enviously. Wait. I have a bag of brisket and fries growing cold. I rip open the bag to create a serving platter.

The server reaches for the bag. "Let me grab you a plate. I could reheat your meal."

"No, I'm good."

"Here. I'll bring you a fresh order of fries."

The server scoops the entire bag and leaves me to gape at the empty table in her wake. She returns a minute later with my brisket and a piping hot bag of fries on a tray. "Anything else?"

"We're good here. Thanks."

Once the server has left, Anja forks two slices of meat onto a taco and tops it with pickled onions and jalapeños plus a healthy squirt of barbecue sauce. "Mmm!"

I hesitate before attacking my meal. She's captivating, even while taking greedy bites of a messy taco. She doesn't throttle her impulses. I envy her ability to dive into everything with curiosity, enthusiasm, and appreciation.

She has unearthed a long-dormant side of me. Mallory might have reminded me I miss having a girlfriend, but it was Anja with whom I bonded.

I finish an oversized bite and wipe my mouth. "I have a confession to make."

CHAPTER 55
ANJA

I pop the last bite of my taco into my mouth. "You were saying?"

"I might have made a wish a week ago. You remember the way I was talking to you when you first arrived tonight?"

"Would it be mean for me to make a joke about your liberal use of the word *talking*?" I press my fingers against my lips to prevent myself from saying anything unkind.

"I deserve it. My magical power pre-tattoo was I could kill a conversation with a single grunt. For some reason, I became Mr. Loquacious after the tattoo. With Mallory; with you. Pretty much any woman I was in contact with over the phone was on the receiving end of unprecedented quantities of words."

"Why do you assume your talkative tendencies resulted from magic?"

"That was my wish: to get to know a woman without having to meet her in person."

I draw a deep breath to buy myself time. He hasn't presented me with an invitation to barge in and make assumptions regarding his reason for his wish. It's his story; I need to give him the page on which to write it. "You're an introvert, right?"

"I am, but introversion is the least of my problems. I've built relationships in the past. Mallory." He flips his hands, presenting exhibit A. "She dumped me before this happened." He rubs his pointer and middle finger from the outside corner of his left eye to his cheekbone. For a second, he drifts somewhere less pleasant. Shaking it off, he says, "I didn't expect the injury to change me. Honestly, *it* didn't. The catalyst was people's reactions to my scar. I had never previously considered how biased humans are toward beauty. Several people treated me as less than because of my face, forcing me into hibernation mode. Staying hidden is safer." He fidgets with his sauce-streaked paper napkin.

"Did you feel more like yourself this week?" I ask.

His smile returns, endowing the asymmetrical upturn of his lips with knee-wobbling powers. "I did. It happened with Mallory and again with a star, the granddaughter of another missing person. I hate myself for putting it this way, but I felt normal."

"You are normal. Well, take that with a grain of salt, because I am no authority on normal. But you were genuine. Talking and texting with you was the only relief I had from drowning in the unrelenting proof that men are scum."

"Our conversations were the most... um, let's say normalizing." His eyes pull mine to his, sending a wave of dizziness into my skull.

Wait. I recognize the dizziness. I had a bout of it... I check my watch. It's two minutes past eight. Figures I'm late.

"I totally spaced the countdown to releasing my tattoo. Hold on."

I rip the tape and bandage from my lower leg. My butterfly opens his wings for me. I had forgotten how vibrant the colors were. The cobalt on the upper wings bleeds into a paler blue, and in the lower wings, the sage green becomes a whisper until it blends in with my skin. The black outlines are intense and precise. And they are a perfect match for the ink on Griffin's arm.

"I'm the sort who'd think nothing of plunking her foot on the table to show you my tattoo, but the holiness of the brisket and pork belly prevents me from going full-Anja on you." I demurely stick my right foot out from under the table. "Nice, huh?"

His fingers threaten to examine the tattoo at closer range. I hold my breath, hoping they will, but he instead lets them twitch from afar. "I had no idea tattoo artists could blend colors. It's insane what they can do with a tattoo machine. And your butterfly is a lovely addition to your ankle. How are the voices?"

Oh, the voices. I push my hands against my stomach to counter the now-familiar adrenaline rush I experience before receiving a flurry of announcements. With a tentative turn of my head, I power up the peepers and take inventory of the men in the restaurant. I catch the eyes of four leering at me, two of whom give me the grin/head nod combination that preceded so many of my unhappy dating adventures. I hear nothing except the churn of conversation and clatter of metal trays shifting on tables and counters.

"They're gone."

It's an enormous relief. I had wondered all week what the voices had actually accomplish for me. They didn't protect me from Colton. They made me double down on my perception that men, in general, suck. And they made me doubt my value as a partner. Only one man was worth meeting, the man I figured I'd never see again. Yet here he is, sitting across from me.

I reach into my bag and pull out the notebook. My fingers pinch its edges. "You want to know what I heard when our eyes met at Inklyn?"

He hugs himself, and his eyes grow round. "I'm not sure."

"Your description is flattering. 'Honest, funny, and values inner beauty.'"

A hint of a satisfied smile gives way to a contemplative frown. Tiny pinprick dimples form under his bottom lip. "Nothing about wanting to add your severed head to my collection in the attic?"

"Do you have an attic?"

"No."

"Then I'm safe. Provided I don't agree to give our friend sitting at two o'clock a try."

"What was his headline?"

"He wants to watch his date and me wrestle in a vat of chocolate pudding."

Griffin's hand smashes against his lips to control his laugh. "It must be a relief not to hear the announcements. Now you can enjoy your beautiful tattoo. I'm a huge fan of mine, so the way I see it, I come out ahead. But after the whole reconnecting with Mallory event, which raised my hopes we'd give our relationship another try, I didn't see the point of carrying on conversations with ease."

"The narration seemed pointless, too. Between my ex and the undesirable stock of men, I figured the lesson for the week was to embrace being single and pour my energy into doing my job more diligently."

Griffin slides his hands between his thighs, drawing his shoulders forward. His eyes shift between mine to the crumbs of meat left behind on his tray. "Every man you encountered was undesirable?"

My impulse is to give him the lump sum of my flirtation techniques by tossing my hair, batting the lashes, and letting him know in no uncertain terms through my body language and innuendo I am his for the offering. I suspect he doesn't speak such language with the same fluency as the men on whom I've employed my techniques in the past. And that could be why my stomach has resumed its fluttering routine. I care more about the outcome than I ever have.

I scrape a shred of meat from between my molars with my pinky nail. "Oh, sorry. Rude. I'm in public." I give my nail an aggressive rub with my napkin.

Griffin holds the packaged moist towelette sitting on the corner of my tray. "A little dental floss would be a better giveaway. I've been wrestling more than my fair share of meat slivers for the last half hour. Unless you want dessert, maybe you can ask for your check. We need to find our way to a private tooth-picking session."

His eyes bounce from left to right. I bite back a smile and wave to our server. Griffin and I don't return to our conversation until I've paid for my meal and we're on the sidewalk.

I scuff the toe of my shoe on the concrete. "To answer your pre-meat-stuck-between-teeth question, not every man was a dud. A single voice might have had the power to raise my hopes."

"Any chance it was from a man who definitely won't chop off your head in the next fourteen hours?" He raises his eyebrows. Sparks dance in his brown eyes in the beam from the streetlight.

I rub the sides of my neck. "So oddly specific. Exactly the sort of comment a serial killer makes in hopes someone will discover his secret. You sure you don't write thrillers?"

"I fare better in the gentle world of steampunk."

"I'm halfway through book two of your newest series. May I declare myself your biggest fan?"

He lowers his head but hangs onto his smile. "You didn't have to read them."

"Oh, but I did. I was a fan of your writing before I knew you were an author. You know how we both wondered whether the wishes we had been granted were worth it? Yours was, for me. Because you led the way, we embarked on the sorts of conversations I had never had with my exes. You asked questions designed for me to reveal myself to you. Nobody I've dated was ever interested in how my mind operates. Or shared the inner workings of his. I know you in a way I've never known a boyfriend. And what I've learned is—" I reach for his hand. He's slow to take mine, but when he does, a tingle originating under my butterfly tattoo migrates to my toes and my fingers and enshrouds me in a sense of luminescence. "We make sense together."

"I haven't made sense with anyone in years. After a few unpleasant reminders during my trip to California, I determined I was done taking responsibility for making people feel okay with my scars. You're different. With you, I don't have to explain myself or apologize for my appearance. You make me…" He bows his head, leaving his thoughts unfinished.

I draw my shoulders to my ears, sensing what he wants to say to me but feeling too shy to complete his sentence for him. "It's unacceptable for anyone to ask you to help them be decent human beings. What my curse taught me is most people aren't for me or you or anyone like us, which is to say folks with depth and awesomeness. We won't connect with most people on the planet."

"I agree. Which is why I can't believe I found you. It's…" Again, the breath of air fueling his words runs low, draining his courage to complete his thought. I need to give him his space, but I'm not sure how much longer I can wait for him to say what I'm longing to hear him say.

"Finding each other was a long shot, one that means the world to me." His eyes meet mine and dart away before he speaks again. "I suppose we should thank our tattoo artists for using the Mystic Mate ink. And Jacob Lowenstein. It took a missing violinist for us to find each other."

"Oh, Mr. Lowenstein! He so needed to be found." I gaze at the amazing man standing in front of me. The tingling within me is unwilling to wait another second. "We could read our pre-prepared acceptance speeches until the orchestra cuts us off, or you could kiss me. Your choice."

With an uncharacteristic burst of decisiveness, he tugs me toward him until I crash against his chest. Letting my hands drop, his fingers brush my hair behind my head. His right hand presses my shoulder blade until I am so close to him, I'm practically behind him. With his left hand cradling my head, his lips find mine.

This isn't the kiss I had expected from a man with a timid streak. Not that I'm disappointed. Quite the opposite. His fervent movements reduce me to a pliant mound of whipped cream. I let my mouth go where his takes it, and my lips expand and contract with his. Our kiss transports me to a place of security, of excitement, of passion I didn't know I possessed. And considering the intensification of the tingle radiating within my body, I know with the utmost certainty our connection, while dosed in magic, has taken on a life of its own now that we are together.

EPILOGUE
ONE MONTH LATER

GRIFFIN

A chilly gust sends the top several pages of my manuscript into the air like oversized snowflakes. I stretch to retrieve them while keeping my left hand on the remaining papers in the stack atop Anja's coffee table.

"Ooh, I should have warned you I was opening the window. Sorry. Give me a second. I need to set mi amigo upright." She fiddles with the mask stuck in the dirt of a window box filled with dead plants.

"We're nearly two weeks past Día de Muertos. Aren't you due to change the display over to Thanksgiving or Christmas?"

With a slam, she closes the window, rearranging the purple tasseled fabric standing in for a set of curtains. "Not until Groundhog Day."

I can't imagine what will appear in her window boxes next, but that's the thrill of living in Anja's world.

Since the breeze has abated, I rearrange the pages and pat them. "All yours."

She sits beside me on the couch, squeezing against me. "Fair warning: the second I tuck into your book, I'm lost to you. You sure you want to compete with your words for my attention?"

"Every shiny object, intriguing sound, or random thought to cross your mind is potential competition for me. But I always win." I noisily kiss the top of her head.

"Then let's declare you the victor once again. I will save your novel for when we're apart."

"What if I never leave your side?"

"I'd be the happiest woman in Jersey City. You could read your book aloud to me. Best of both worlds."

I scratch my eyebrow. "I've never asked any friends or family members to read an early draft. For good reason. It's terrifying. I'd rather not be in the room while you read it."

"You're safe with me." She snuggles into my side, resting her head on my shoulder.

She's not wrong.

"Since you're not going to read my draft, what should we do? Perhaps pay Mr. Lowenstein a visit?"

"He is always at his most alert listening to music. Out of respect to those who observe the Sabbath, I don't play guitar on Saturdays. And they also frown upon the use of electronic devices. Let's save his visit for tomorrow. He is surrounded by photos and memorabilia from his career. I bet he is listening to tangos in his head without us."

"Then what do you suggest?"

"We could make out." She straddles my legs and bends her head toward me. Her hair falls between us, tickling my face. Her hands corral it into a ponytail. "Better?"

Her phone rings. She bunches her eye. I say, "Get it. I'll still be here."

She bounds off my lap toward the kitchen counter, where she left her phone after breakfast.

"Tracey! What's shaking?"

Anja slides her back against the kitchen's doorframe, lowering herself into a squat.

"Aw, honey, I'm sorry. Do you want to come over and talk?"

She holds her finger in the air to let me know she'll be awhile.

"Take a breath. It's your first time back on the horse. It will get better. It did for me"

She nods while listening to her friend.

"I suppose a tattoo would keep your mind off of it…. Where? Um, a place near Violet's…. There are loads of other places. Perhaps one near you? … Sure, Amelia is amazingly talented, but I don't want you following my footsteps. This is your journey, remember? … Fine. I went to Inklyn. But perhaps you should stay away from an ink… You know what? You do you. And I'm here for you, no matter what. You are ten thousand different kinds of wonderful. You deserve to find your happiness again. I believe in you, my friend…. I love you, too. Call me the second you make a decision, you hear? … Bye!"

Anja presses herself to her feet and returns to the couch. "Tracey had one doozy of a bad first date last night. Anyway, she took my advice to distract herself while she recovers. She wants a tattoo."

"Did I hear you warning her away from following in our exact tattoo experience footsteps?"

"At first, yeah. But look at the evidence in favor of her making a wish on magical tattoo ink. Ben and Violet swapped bodies, wound up with better jobs, and fell in love. Worth it, right?"

I plant a kiss on her lips. "Aren't you forgetting two other inked people?"

"I saved the best for last, babe. You saved me from hammering my misfit peg into the wrong hole. Sometimes I imagine the alternate reality where you weren't at Inklyn. I would have made my wish, would not have heard your inner truth, and you would have contacted me to enlist my aid in locating León Roca without the ability to carry on interesting, revealing conversations with me."

"But that's not how our story goes."

"Exactly. Tracey needs her happy ending. Were I to steer her away from Amelia and her magical ink, she might not find hers."

"Here's to happy endings, then." I knock Anja backwards on the couch and lean over her. "You promised me we'd make out. I've come to collect."

She laughs and pulls me to her. "Show me what you got."

Easier done than said.

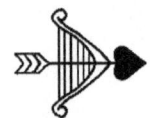

Thank you so much for taking the time to read *Found Together*. I hope you'll share your review on Amazon, Goodreads and/or Bookbub to let new readers know what you thought about this book.

The tattoo ink continues to grant wishes. Experience its magic in the final book of the series, *Back Together*.

Magical ink. Two wishes. Now Tracey and Jayden have a second chance.

Tracey Byrne is ready for a new relationship a year after her fiancé cheated on her, but one horrible first date later, spinsterhood is looking better than ever.

Jayden Mitchell wants to restart his life. But sleeping on a friend's couch and putting off signing his divorce papers is holding up progress.

When he and Tracey, his college girlfriend, reunite, they wish they could go back in time to fix their problems. Not literally, though.

Now they're stuck five years in the past and in danger of rewriting history. According to the calendar, they haven't met yet, which is inconvenient when old desires become new again.

After Jayden reconnects with the one person he hoped he'd never see again—his soon-to-be ex-wife—and Tracey questions the choices she made in college, their official reunion seems doomed before it happens. Can they fix their mistakes and save each other before it's too late to return to the future?

THANK YOU:

Writing novels is ninety percent sitting alone in a room, a good seven percent spent asking Google questions sure to confuse any forensic experts who might ever check my search history, and at least fifty percent support from my peeps. Wait. That adds up to over one hundred. But that's how it works. Without the guidance I receive from these people, I could never reach the end of a book.

For all things Dorothy DeLay, I turned to my colleague, Denise, one of her former students, and to her mother Elaine, the original wrangler of Miss DeLay's schedule. I thank both of you from the bottom of my heart for sharing your knowledge!

My beta team once again steered me toward a polished draft. Thank you, Kirsty and Karolyn!

My sister Heidi captured Anja and Griffin perfectly on the cover. And to hear her tell it, I haven't yet driven her nuts with my incessant input on what else we can do with the design.

Finally, there is Kevin, who has withstood eighteen months of captivity with me, complete with blow-by-blow accounts of the minutia of an author's life (no one needs to hear half of what I share) and my continued grumblings regarding the never-ending need to keep the two of us fed. One day soon, we'll return to our previously scheduled lives as busy musicians, and when that happens, I know coming home to you will be the highlight of my day.

ALSO BY DIANE MICHAELS

Novels
The Inked Together Series
Inked Together
Found Together
Back Together

The Empire State of Mind Series
Splitting Heirs
Last Resort
Home Cooking
Keyed Up
Date Bloomer

The Ellen the Harpist Series
Ellen the Harpist
Ellen at Sea
Ellen the Bride

A Christmas Rescue
Pet Peeves

Novellas
King & Queen of the Bouncy Castle
King & Queen of the Roller Derby
King & Queen of the Bowling Alley
King & Queen of the Poker Game
King & Queen of the Carnival

Short Stories
Watching the Grass Grow

Wedding Ceremony Music Guide
From Here Comes the Bride to There Go the Grooms

Visit http://dianemichaelsbooksandharp.com to view her sheet music for harp.

ABOUT THE AUTHOR

Diane Michaels is a harpist and author. She balances her fondness for ice cream with her enjoyment of working out and walking through the woods. When she is not spying on the world from behind her harp to collect ideas for her next book, she and her husband make up stories and songs for and about their miniature poodle, Lola.

You can learn more about Ms. Michaels at http://dianemichaelsbooksandharp.com